Are they honouring time for being so tender a killer?
—Rainer Maria Rilke

"Scandalous, beautifully tawdry, lyrical noir. A steady pulse of accomplished, phantasmagoric prose elevates this lurid tale above standard crime fare. So Tender a Killer is that bitter 90-minute thriller on sketchy late night TV you feel you could get in trouble for watching."

— Jesse Hilson (Author, *Blood Trip* and *The Tattletales*)

"So Tender a Killer is Jim Thompson meets Anna Kavan for a sundae on Mars. Matthew Kinlin brilliantly creates a queasy, dreamy, nightmarish vision that's addictive. It reminds me of reading Muriel Spark––the dread but also the lingering details, a way of looking that is seductive and repellant and recognizable. Right from the first line and page––'I liked to pour my body inside the envy of others,' Vanessa, the narrator, is so magnetic and perfectly sane in the way that the truly insane always are."

— Nate Lippen (Author, *Ripcord*, and *My Dead Book*)

"The prose in Matthew Kinlin's new novel is so pleasurable to read, it washes over you like the purest spring, leaving your imagination feeling dewy and salved. Some of these sentences are so moreish, I treated myself — reading them over and over. The work is elegantly restrained but bolstered by a beautiful poetic heartbeat. So Tender a Killer is Kinlin's greatest, strongest work so far."

— Thomas Moore (Author, *Alone* and *Your Dreams*)

So Tender a Killer
Copyright © 2025 Matthew Kinlin
Book & cover design by Ira Rat

This is a work of fiction. Names, characters, businesses, places, events, locales, and incidents are either the products of the author's imagination or used in a fictitious manner. Any resemblance to actual persons, living or dead, or actual events is purely coincidental.

This book may not be reproduced in whole or in part, except for the inclusion of brief quotations in a review, without permission in writing from the author or publisher. No part of this publication may be reproduced, stored in or introduced into retrieval system, or transmitted, in any form, or by any means (electronic, mechanical, photocopying, recording, or otherwise), without prior permission of the publisher.

Requests for permission should be directed to filthylootpress@gmail.com

FIRST EDITION

SO TENDER A KILLER

MATTHEW KINLIN

TALENTED PERVERTS

filthyloot.com

Celine, my dream is to watch you die.

1.

It was the brightest day of spring when I decided to buy a gun. I was undressing before a golden reflection in the mirror on the opposite wall. Mercurial, in a hot fountain of light, I walked from one end of the room to the other. I was like a kingfisher on fire.

There was the light, and the mirror, and the tulips on the dresser. My hand reached for a bottle of Evian beneath their green and broken throats. Eventually, I emptied the water into the bowl of flowers. I felt cleaner sat near to them. As the day went on, the smell of the tulips became stronger and more intense. The leaves were faded, their petals chalky. I wanted them to suffer because they smelled sweeter as they died.

There was an opened box on the hotel bed. Folded neatly inside was a black dress that Cate Blanchett recently wore in Madrid. I only bought it because it made the shop assistant jealous. I could see the way she looked at me when I asked for her opinion, the plasma rising in her face like a sharp orange crescent. I liked to pour my body inside the envy of others. Over the last decade, fashion designers stitched their resentments to my skin. They saw me as nothing but a mosaic of contempt, an unconscious projection which they hacked at madly with scissors and thread, handfuls of red shameful silk. Mute and alone, I remained very still. A pathetic marionette bombarded on its little metal stand. Breathless, I peeled off their clothes behind paper screens backstage. I saw my own body as a silver aircraft. It was easier to think of myself as a machine.

There were weeks when I wanted no one to touch me. I drew a simple pink line around my reflection. It was like living inside a powerful forcefield. I repelled the attractions of others through mental electromagnetism. I carried this negative fury with me like bright tumours that burned through the skin.

Back at the hotel, I ordered room service, a small Greek salad and a little fruit. The balcony outside was covered in pigeon droppings. London was an enormous decadent tomb. The rich swam through its columned streets like paramedics throwing white roses at the feet of paparazzi. For a moment, I considered returning to the shopping arcade but remembered the assistant attacking me with clouds of men's cologne, the smell of leather, and grilled cigarettes. Escalators: perfect transition from earth into air. Rays of sunlight stretched and refracted as they sank through the crystal rooftop into the carpark. The faceless driver was sat waiting in the Uber. His shadow followed me through the hotel lobby, shimmering along the parquet floor. It carried with it the silence of bees as they kneaded their own siblings into honey. I needed to stop thinking, so distracted myself by scrolled through images on my phone. Balenciaga. Chanel. Haunted twinks that resembled French lilac ghosts. A photograph of Taipei sunk beneath silver pollution. A sightless Italian carcass floating on a pond of watercress.

Listening to the London traffic, choral through the sealed balcony doors, I thought again of my daughter back in Winchester. It was the day we visited the reptile house. The inside walls of the concrete shell were pebbled in lizard shit. She had pleaded for an hour to buy a milk snake. I could see my daughter's face under the strong heat lamps. She resembled a bright red worm. Finally, we took the creature home. And four days later, in one opulent shudder, it burst through its own skin. The following afternoon, I found a photograph of Celine behind my dressing table, and every mirror in the house shattered.

I was filled with slowness. A hot white zero in the first light of spring. My confusion surrendered to something pale and alone, an exhaustion that lifted me on further. I had constant migraines. Delirious, I saw myself falling through the atmosphere of some distant planet. I had the awful dreams of a magnesium statue shattering on the surface of Jupiter. At night, I crawled into my daughter's bedroom and saw the snake asleep inside its trapezoid case. I remembered its metamorphosis, the uncanny repetition of itself. Before a snake begins to shed its skin, its eyes turn blue and slowly begin to cloud.

The sun came roaring through the whole house the next morning. It bounded up and down the hallway like a stupid dog. Golden, it knocked on each and every door. With its lolling tongue, it painted all of our bodies in bright shadows. Our dreams came to nothing when faced with the idiocy of the sun. Sat across from my husband, he suddenly resembled a bald watermelon. We became embarrassed when making love. It felt like taking out the rubbish. Where once there was intimacy, there was now only humiliation. I grew to accept and live inside this space. There were days when I looked at my children, and all I saw was their hatred and selfishness. Silently, I learned to digest my revulsion of them as easily as spaghetti. I was patient and took my time to cut my disgust into very fine pieces. I smiled at them from across the table.

The light in the house was like a tuning fork. I held it closely to my ear, where it confessed secrets kept only for me because a secret is a luxury of the lonely. Light formed a shadow along the sill of the bedroom window. It stood in alignment with a polar opposite that could never be reconciled. An unknown pair of surgical hands drew a blue equinox down my face. The shadow on the windowsill conveyed a dream that passed across a pale meridian. The blank expressions of furniture. In the garden at dusk, I inhaled handfuls of cold English dirt. I thought once more of fucking Celine, her face and ass glowing with spit.

As I turned to face the automatic shape in the hotel mirror, light continued to flood through the hand of another organism that resembled a bird or an effigy. A scarecrow scattered like black geometry across the laminate flooring as I moved towards the glass. An image overflowing with the cold joy of metal. An assassin. A nightcrawler riddled with quicksilver skin. Everything must suffer. My revenge would be sick and sweet. I was patient and let it purr softly in my lap. I was like a delirious phantom stood in silent doorways. It was then I saw everything in the hotel room clearly. The key turned slowly in the lock. The tulips floating in their bowl. The dress on the unmade bed.

2.

Blue endless night. The entrance to the hotel stood before me, cavernous and emptied of itself: a disembowelled Victorian chamber erected over a century ago. In the centre of the rectangular lobby stood a single statue on top of a marble plinth. A stone child looked upwards with pale eyes into the blasted ether of London fog. The smooth bust of the boy was brindled in dust. The plinth swam inside lavender gloam beneath the brittle moonlight. Its solemn presence transfixed me. His hands had broken off into branches of chalk.

The revolving doors reversed in the cold draft as traffic lights switched from amber into green. The moonlight poured thickly down through the glass atrium but swiftly changed direction, reflecting off the feline bodies of cars as they rushed through the junction. Slowly, the dark shadow of the statue grew along the wall into a new shape. His body had arched and elongated itself like a Grecian witch, crooked chin pointing to the front desk where a disingenuous concierge held a phone near to his chin. His manner was nimble and elegant. I could tell he was homosexual: the glowing layers of sarcophagi makeup on his face, the way the burlesque death mask twitched as I tapped at my watch. He stabbed at the keyboard like a swan feeding on grubs. I took a seat and waited for him to order a taxi.

As the pink moon began to fade softer, the traffic became almost invisible and sank into the ground. All that remained was the statue of the child in an abandoned city. Cupid—blind orphan of misfortune. Eventually, a dazed horizon formed above its shoulders. I thought of floating through dark currents at the blank ends of the Antarctic. Radioactive surfaces like planets dragged through auroras of green crescents above melting ice. A pale shimmer rose above the head of the boy when I caught my own reflection in the polished surface beneath the marbled reception. In my enormous Burberry trench-coat, I resembled a large Alsatian dog. My face carried the distorted shape of an animal. The clouds outside were moving across the sky.

Irritated, the concierge continued to pass the phone from his left to his right hand. His nose twitched again like a rodent before finally he hung up. I rose from the oxblood Chesterfield in a tower of umber.

"A taxi, madam?" he asked in a false, effeminate voice.

"Yes, please."

"Right away."

I flashed a smile, and the concierge mirrored with a weak and automatic grimace before dialling the number.

Walking towards the revolving door, the heels of my shoes danced through the multiplying shadows of the plinth, kaleidoscopic across the marble-veined floor. As the door span open, the darkness deepened around the base of the plinth into a roulette wheel of broken oblong shapes. A constellation, obsidian to pale grey: soft, confessing marble.

The taxi swam fluently through the empty streets. We complied with its silent fulcrums of corrupt money, a district carved into chalk alcoves, glowing caves of hollowed limestone. The streets were filled with white Georgian mansions, all populated with only one or two souls, whilst the other huge rooms lay empty. Like slender men, the lampposts projected their own shadows across the pavements of the roads we weaved through. An indigo warren. We passed a Victorian pub painted in ultramarine on a street corner. Stopping at a traffic light, I noticed an art gallery filled with canvases of Cy Twombly. Some were covered in acrylic streaks. Others had long graphite coils of electricity that ran through the spattered mess. I thought for a moment of my own children presenting me with work from personal notebooks: a doodle of life on some obscene planet. They mistook my silence for maternal confidence. Walking towards the large American-style refrigerator, I took out of a large bottle of carbonated juice and poured it blindly into their sticky, clapping hands.

"Here is fine."

"Are you sure, ma'am?" the driver asked, gently pushing on the brake, "Hyde Park is only a few minutes away."

"I know where we are. It's such a nice night. I'd like to walk a little," I replied, handing him the money and waving away the change.

"Well, if you insist, ma'am. And thank you, that's very generous."

Closing the door, I watched the vehicle move along the cobbled street. The city felt vast and deserted. The stone walls of the avenue were possessed with a vibrant brio. Even the cheap tarmac shone. As I walked towards the entrance of the park, I zig-zagged my index finger across the cold external railings. Soon, I came to a brick wall hidden beneath the dark English ivy. My heart began to flutter madly inside my chest like the wings of a frightened chicken. I slowed my breathing. I told myself to relax. Some nights require patience. I tried to relish the moment as

I wandered beneath the archway of the park and floated across its dew-jewelled, exquisite lawns. Before meeting the stranger at the lake, I stopped to admire the cobalt ducks huddled together, asleep on the freezing bank.

Even the spiders were coming out from behind the pale petals of daffodils to reveal their twilit innocence, lost inside bright folds of gossamer. I found great pleasure in this sense of delay. I glanced at the blue darkness above. One must choose the correct moment, at the quietest hour of night, to reach down into the cold water. An executioner staring at blank constellations. The stars were slow in their own extinction.

At the bench we had agreed, the stranger was dressed as exactly as he described: red baseball cap, Adidas trainers. He was younger than I had imagined. His face thin and sunken at the cheeks. A scar indicated a cleft lip.

"I have the money," I said quickly, sitting myself down.

"Give it to me then," he replied, brusquely with a thick, muffled accent.

"I need to see it."

I could hear rustling in his jacket as he fumbled with a plastic bag. From inside, he pulled out the revolver. He handed it to me so I could feel it. It sat heavy for a few seconds in my lap. It seemed almost like a toy, except for the weight. Inside the plastic bag, there was also a small cardboard box of bullets. Silently, I handed him a roll of bank notes I had taken from the ATM that morning. As a model working in London, you meet many cocaine dealers, and you sense the ones that have connections. The stranger took his time to count the money carefully. He began to smile.

"You sure look scared, lady."

Nodding, I silently got up from the bench.

Behind me, I could hear the boy laughing.

With rehearsed ease, as though I was in a play or a film, I simply placed the revolver and bullets inside my purse and made my way back through the park. I only stopped once to glance through the windows of the pavilion, which was filled with exotic plants drowned in warm shade.

A Jurassic palm tree spanned the entire building with voracious, ancient limbs. Behind the nearest window, a single white orchid floated in mid-air like a phantom. The stark lip of its petal had softened into a crease of mauve blood. The night suddenly turned cold. I could feel my hand on the gun was shaking.

3.

The hallway of the apartment looked exactly the same. Corridors moved into rooms of the past. Days and months and years had submerged into objects, engrained themselves inside the green-black front door, the same, thick and inviting wool carpet. Nailed to the inside wall was the Lebanese rug we bought in Baalbek. An illicit affair reduced to a few souvenirs. After eight whole years, the rug resembled a butterfly rising in clouds of doubt. Its blue silken thorax was filled with peppery scythes that formed undulating waves, a sequence of concentric lines which, in the weak light of the hallway, now resembled smoke: a perfect X on the wall, a signal billowing from a faraway valley. Crystalline. A blue Okinawa omen.

The apartment remained immaculate, as it always was. The strawberry thief cushion waited in an upstairs room: a fat bird trapped in bracken. Nervously, I felt for the shape of the revolver in the purse. I was relieved to glide my finger softly along the outline of its cylinder. The weapon was lodged in the front pocket of the purse. During last winter, I had dreamed of an animal draped across Celine's bed, a female fox or a wolf. Its dark and shining fur. Its purple hole spread apart.

This place had always been a sanctuary. It invited its own calming etiquette. I sensed that the years had passed by exactly the same as before, like a beautiful masquerade: pots of green gnocchi boiling in the kitchen in basil-sweet smoke, other women embraced in the hallway, red pinot noir spilling through a veneered gap tooth. Celine had lived a charmed life. It was she like reached inside her own mouth as a child and found an immaculate key. Shelves in the hallway were filled with small photographs in silver Asprey frames. I walked towards the image. She had her arms wrapped around a beautiful Bichon Frise. I didn't know the dog and resented it instantly. At the end of the hallway was the huge Henri Cartier-Bresson print she bought in Pamplona: an infant in a white smock dragging itself across a rotting wall. Its eyes were turned towards the ceiling, lost endlessly in the delirium of its small and limitless mind.

I held the gun trembling before me. I turned from the hallway into the living room. I recognised her in a matter of seconds. She was sat facing the television. And in that moment, I remembered when we first met in the south of Spain, in an Andalusian fortress on the Iberian Peninsula. It was my second year of modelling for international clients.

That was over fifteen years ago now. Even in the early hours of the morning, the temperature had been intergalactic. From the caravan door, I watched a vibrating wall of heat float above the wasteland before I levitated towards the mirrored photoshoot. The Leipzig office had hired Celine Stein, a big name in the industry. She stood before me in her masculine Lacoste polo and asked me to hold the birdcage higher. I was shaking on the castle walls in the midday sun in an ivory Alexander McQueen gown. Inside the birdcage were three Philippian kingfishers. Each bird had a red face, and orange bodies streaked in bright markings. A representative from Mercedes was trying to speak with Celine, who she batted away like an insect. I marvelled at her confidence as she marched proudly in the dazzling courtyard of the castle.

Alcazaba of Almeria. Clear water reflected and caught across the tails of clairvoyant birds. The animal trainer had brought a pair of turquoise peafowls to set. The other models were struggling, with patches of sweat appearing on their heavier, yellow corsets. Finally, desperate but hopeful, Celine signalled for me to stand alone on the fortress wall and hold up the cage one more time. The kingfishers suddenly burst into a series of piercing calls and flung their wings open. Looking into the distance, I could make out cyclones of sand rising through the air like hysterical djinns invoking the azure strip of water beyond. I could hear the camera echoing through the ancient ruins. Our weak bodies became lost amongst birdsong, their terrified screams. That photo made the cover and made my entire career. It was a manifestation of the phantasmagorical birds.

That night, we made love back at the hotel.

Celine removed her shirt and jeans. I reached towards the shape, moving through the room. She smelled like acrid sweat. Her flesh was hard and stonelike. A southern African moon fell through the translucent canopy above the bed. The sheets were covered in blind dragonflies. When she touched me, an exquisite feeling of coldness ran through my entire body. Every night was like a grave in which we buried ourselves in secrecy. Our lips were touching. She swallowed my breath. She ate through my body like wallpaper: a distant and amber palimpsest that I learned to call *skin*.

Drifting from the hallway into the living room, past the Henri Cartier-Bresson print, I held the gun towards the immobile victim on the sofa nearest to the television. I knew for sure it was Celine's head. She was directly facing the television. The sofa had been moved. It was on the left side of the room, whereas before, it had been beneath the large Georgian window, facing the door. Unusually, the floor was scattered with books and magazines gathered around the base of the sofa where Celine was sat with her feet resting on the coffee table. She wore white trainer socks. Even from the back of her head, I could see she had changed. Her striking silver hair had faded to grey. As she lifted the large glass of red wine to her mouth, I noticed the wrinkles in her hands had deepened. She had the hands of an old woman. And yet, from the side, her face appeared the same. It was still tight and beautiful.

Shaking, I walked towards the sofa. The image on the television screen was a news reporter inside a luminous studio. I placed the gun to the back of Celine's head.

I couldn't recall any noise. There was no sound of the gun going off. There was just the soft click of the safety being pulled back and then a long period of stillness afterwards. I never heard the gunshot or the sound of the bullet moving through Celine's head. I never heard it emerge from the front of her face into the wine glass or the bullet ricocheting off the south-facing wall into the windowpane. The bullet had simply flown away. The murder was a quiet and simple act, like diving into a clear stretch of water.

Afterwards, there was only the width of the silence. It was like when you tilted your head to one side after swimming and the whole world floods back inside. The television presenter on the screen continued to speak. I could hear loud footsteps on the floor above. It was only then that I saw a dark smear across the wall. I ran from the room and soon was in the hallway and out the front door that Celine never locked until bedtime, back onto the street. I didn't run but walked briskly, making sure to put the revolver back inside my purse in the dark alleyway at the side of the house. Not looking backwards, I made my way down the Highgate hill. I saw a large bus pulling up to the stop opposite. I sat on the top deck amongst drunken passengers making their way home. They laughed and jeered as rain built softly on the windows of the vehicle. I watched neon streams of traffic as they navigated the city. Fluorescent lines converged at a junction that fractured outwards into bright webs of shivering vectors. The cars swam down the dark arterial road.

4.

Sailing towards and through. Sailing through and under the blue alcoves of the airport entrance, I eventually came to a pair of automatic doors that chimed open at the distant rumble of footsteps. Somehow, the glass sensed the figures that moved towards them. The doors listened calmly and without judgement to the explosions of aeroplanes as they flung themselves upwards into bright black heaven.

It was daybreak. The lower half of the sky had begun to rupture into violet and then pale ash. Standing at the edge of the walkway, I watched amber light filter through the base of concrete blocks that ran alongside the eastern runway. The first light broke beyond the estuary, out towards Holland, Germany, the frozen limb of Denmark sunk beneath the sea. Holding my breath, I placed my toiletries delicately inside their plastic bag. There was an intimacy to these items, which I entrusted my body with every day, the remains of what I could salvage from the hotel room: a bottle of Elizabeth Arden concealer, Carolina Herrara red matte lipstick. Before leaving, I rubbed half the entire bottle of concealer across my face and neck. My hands were sweating in brown prints as I covered the upper level of skin. It was like wearing another face. When I applied makeup, I liked to pretend I was sinking through the surface of an enormous beach of the finest volcanic sand. I disappeared beneath its bitter minerals. Afterwards, I asked the concierge to phone my second taxi of the night.

Sealing the plastic bag, I walked through the security gate, where I was bombarded by walls of invisible radiation. I imagined its waves rippling across the contours of my flesh beneath the black Chanel dress. It was like swimming inside a spacecraft. Suddenly, a red light came on the overhead frame. A woman in a uniform asked me to hold up my arms, which I did obediently as she scanned my torso and legs with a piece of technology that resembled a badminton racquet. I could smell the ionic radiation crashing through my bones, kissing the paper of my lungs. Looking at the monitor screen, there were heat-sensitive images of my belongings inside the hand luggage. Images that resembled maps, the topography of mountainous Pacific islands: bright red velocities, orange, blue, yellow. A small dark shape on the screen suddenly filled me with dread. *Had I emptied all the bullets from the purse?*

"Can you remove your bracelet, miss?" the officer asked, signalling to the Omega steel chain I was wearing.

"Of course," I replied, relief rushing over me. Silently, I placed the jewellery on the moving conveyor, before walking again through the scanner, this time without interruption.

The officer looked me dead in the eyes. I smiled because I was like an artificial continent, one of those beaches they built in Dubai. Endless shopping malls made from zirconium.

I had dumped the gun before the airport. There is a quiet part of Dagenham, down by the water. I used to live there when I started working as a model. Before I met Celine. There was a deserted plot of land that had been taken over by a number of factories and a Norwegian chemical plant. Getting off the bus, I followed the towers of billowing smoke. The air was thick with poison. There were only a few parked cars belonging to men working overnight. A bald, porky man sat in a portacabin at the side of the road. I didn't make eye contact. Just headed past the gates down to the edge of the Thames. Quickly, I tossed the gun into the dark water and tipped the bullets out. The water was filled with toxins, a type of rubber they manufactured in the plant. In that moment, I made a pact with the poison in exchange for my secret. I opened my mouth and breathed in its fumes like a pale psychopomp, my empty hands floating above the fetid water. I sold my worthless soul to the river.

There were no bullets left in the handbag. The purse and sealed toiletries had made its way through the x-ray machine. Moving to the end of the conveyor, I took my bags and exited through further glass screens that led passengers into the departures lounge. There was a long corridor of goods: perfume, chocolates, other luxuries—a tall blue bottle of Scottish gin. The flight ticket was inside my handbag. Back at the hotel, I had scrolled through available seats that morning. I now saw my husband and children waking in their beds. Their expressions were blank and empty. They wandered from room to room like automata. I saw the annex we built onto the back of the Berkshire house slowly filling with morning light.

Last year, the children had bought a goldfish and neglected to feed it. Within weeks it had died. It glowed brightly as it floated clockwise, then anti, on the surface on the dirty water. The corpse of the fish was bronze. The children couldn't even be bothered to acknowledge its passing. As I walked past the rows of vodka bottles, I thought of the dark smear across the wall of Celine's apartment. It was like an unknown piece of Arabic script.

The departures lounge was sparse and empty. The floor had been polished and reflected the shapes of passengers as they wandered along its windowless walls. An old woman wheeled a carry-on case through thin tributaries of people. Her face had broken into a hurricane of green blood vessels. At a large glass door, a handsome man in a dark suit looked silently out at the runways. I stopped to check the departures board.

The flight was on time.

09.48am FLIGHT 46YX to LAS.

It took over ten hours to get from London to Las Vegas. I could see the security guards standing at each side of the lounge. Following closely behind the handsome man, I walked to a kiosk at the far end and rattled through a rack of cheap sunglasses. My face was framed in the mirror at the top as I selected a pair of aviators and paid the man with cash, squirting my hands afterwards with alcohol fluid. Calmly, I walked towards the ATM and accessed the joint account. I took everything I could.

Walking back towards the departures board, I stopped to watch the morning sun rise along the stationary planes. The aeroplanes had flown from city to city, across every continent, and seen nothing. You could sense their exhaustion. The universe offered no rewards to the machines it resurrected.

The old woman was stood now in the centre of the longue. She turned to face the sun. She was a misbegotten shape. She harboured the polished surface of a chess piece—a blue and faceless bishop. Amber sunglow began to flood through the enormous glass wall, obliterating the white suitcase at her feet, climbing the face of its meek pontiff. And suddenly, without warning, the woman was engulfed in her own towering refusal. The expiration of *this* into *then*. The flight was boarding.

5.

Seat 34F. I should have booked first class. The economy chair looked like a plastic hunchback glued to the wall. Sitting patiently, I folded my butter-brown suede gloves inside the purse where the revolver once slept. The hirsute surface of the gloves anticipated our ascent as the calf hair froze, frightened with friction, glowed now softly in the sidereal morning light coming through the right of the stationary plane. Small, hurried shapes in orange hi-vis were loading towers of plastic suitcases inside the abdomen of the behemoth. A low wall of grey cloud rose behind the workers, their faces becoming blurred and indistinguishable from one another like small knots of consciousness.

A head opened suddenly into a pumpkin, a surprised and round O, as it dropped a large case from a moving trolley.

Eventually, a sign above lit up. The ceiling felt too close to my face. I was locked inside. Thankfully, there was no one sat next to me, just the old woman from the departures lounge, perched on the aisle seat. She had laid out magazines in the seat between us, forming a barricade of celebrity gossip, salacious adultery, a pair of bald, baby-bird soap opera gangsters from Essex.

Looking over her insipid literature, the golden face of the elderly woman became lost in a glowing stream of white hair like egg yolk running through the rhythm of a weak and clear albumen. A single hair coiled above the peak of her forehead where the flesh had folded over itself at the boundary of her thin damaged scalp. Raising her hand, she smoothed down the hairline and took a deep breath, steadying herself before moving the handbag from between her legs behind the pile of papers.

"Feel free to read any of these," she said, smiling for a moment.

"That's very kind," I lied, glancing over the large and uncomfortable sunglasses, hoping, *praying*, she was not wanting to make small talk for the next ten hours.

Turning to face the small nozzle on the back of the chair that held the tray upright, I closed my eyes as we prepared to take off. It was the first time I had considered the body of Celine. *Did she fall onto her side? Or did she land face-down in a pool of spinal fluid?* I thought of the bullet in the gun as simply a remote control held to the nape of her neck that, when I pressed the button, flooded the body into evergreen darkness. The red wine in her hand toppled and rushed across the ochre Holland & Sherry rug. Blood was spreading through the expanse of her fingertips flung apart like the faux theatrical wings of a swan, blasted at the exact moment of liquorice impact.

The mouth of the traffic conductor widened again as the plane began to scream into life. The machine reversed backwards from negative death into fire. Purse-lipped, homosexual attendants told us to remain in our seats, politely reminding us of the emergency exits located at each end of the aisle. We moved slowly across the runway, then suddenly jolted forward, a deep rumble that forced me to tighten my eyes shut. I saw the plane as a black curtain pulled upward from the ground. When I opened them again, there was only dazzling blue outside and an occasional patch of sheep white clouds in the morning sky.

The relief was enormous to see the Atlantic, so I ordered myself a beaker of cheap chardonnay. And then another. I held my breath and chucked them down. I was leaving the jurisdiction of British soil, a feudal marshland sinking into the Irish Sea. The water was dancing in brittle constellations. Overwhelmed, I tried to take a series of deep breaths. I thought about the gun sinking into the Thames.

The revolver had led me from door to door. I remembered the feeling of it in my hand. It was like being in a video game. Doors flung open for me on their own accord when I held the weapon. The gun was a divination rod moving towards a screaming oesophagus.

I remembered about nine years ago, snorting powerful cocaine off Celine's coffee table whilst her brother, a social worker battling with his own substance abuse, was playing a Japanese shooter game on the television. Every time you shot someone, you collected their blood. A red cloud rose up from the body you had just slaughtered. It was called *Killer 7*. The blood of your victim riddled you and made you richer. You collected the blood of others like precious jewels.

The wine was going to my head because I started to feel ecstatic. A sharp and wonderful migraine ran down and into my lower jaw. I felt the pressure of the cabin lower as we tilted through the stratosphere. I relished the atmospheric drift, and the suede gloves glowed again with sickly splendour of sunlit murdered calves. The old woman's skull shone through the skin. Translucent and fulgid marrow, a skeleton sent through the sky. All these elements conjoined in my drunken mind to form a medieval conspiracy. I laid them out before me on a stone table and married them inside the pain of the migraine. I was rising into the clouds like a corkscrew moving through a glass bottle.

I was certain Celine must have heard the safety on the gun being pulled back. There was a slight millisecond when she must have known what was about to happen. The migraine in the aeroplane was linked to that fraction of information. The nerve throbbing in my face was a connection between myself and Celine. She knew what she deserved. Celine understood in her deepest heart that I would destroy her.

And yet, it was like I was waiting for it all to happen.

She might be stood in a kitchen somewhere in Putney, cooking rice or pasta on an oven hob. She has her back turned to a steamed window where I am stood. Behind the glass, I am waiting to murder her in some rain-soaked yard. I am lost in grey clouds of condensation.

Patience was my goddess. The dream was yet to come. I wanted her to wake up so I could kill again. I wanted to fill her face with so many holes. She was like an infinity of meat. The migraine in my head was the acceptance of this pleasure, its jarring freedom in my mind. A freezing cold spoon placed inside my mouth.

6.

I found the cleanest motel I could at short notice in this xerothermic dust bowl. A land of cockroaches and atomic-detonated ruins. There's a shame engrained in the faces of people here: the gamblers, the addicts, the hookers, and the rubbernecking tourists in the streets. This is the realm of ghosts dissolving in dark and endless ranchos. I chose Las Vegas because I wanted to be inducted into invisibility.

Las Vegas. The buildings glowed like aluminium UFOs. We drove from the airport towards the shape of a granite pyramid. An Egyptian curse rising into the air, a black tulip. We passed roadside minarets of emerald wealth. Ruined faces of methamphetamine use. Homeless men and women negotiated themselves through downtown alleyways. They swam into labyrinthine supermarkets, the many-mirrored arms of death, blue Vishnu. A woman sold cigarettes from a shopping cart and souvenirs of Taxco silver. Breathless from the heat and pollution of the traffic, I watched elderly diabetic tourists from the window of the taxi fainting under Grecian pillars of a McDonalds. Sex workers with arched and thin shoulders. Las Vegas was like landing on another planet.

The heat of the place sent your mind backwards and forwards through time like a Soviet star mission, the human brain trying to receive oxygen as you levitated out of the tinfoil cabin of the aeroplane.

Sunset Creek Motel was slightly north-west of downtown. It stood at the fringe of the desert, near to the freeway that led up towards Dry Lake and Crystal, before pure extinction, nothing but sand and blank zephyr, rows of pale bracken and lime cacti beneath a grey and immutable sky. I could smell the thundercloud of another migraine condensing inside my skull as the taxi rolled up to the gigantic fluorescent sign in the parking lot constructed from long loops of halogen pipes that promised access to HBO and ESPN. A microwave and wi-fi in every room. The terracotta roof was balding in dark patches of indigo ferns where the tiles had dislodged over a number of years since falling into disrepair. The main building was a blinding tower block of concrete and glass. From the back hung tessellating rows of flamingo pink balconies looking over a swimming pool that shook and reformed in the Nevada light like an electrical jellyfish. Vents at each side blew streams of bubbles through the chlorinated plasma. The surface of the pool was painful to look at in the mid-afternoon glare, especially through the cheap sunglasses. I had to turn away as I pulled open the patio doors and made my way towards the reception desk, dragging the suitcase from the boot of the taxi and waving the driver, Miguel, away.

During the drive, Miguel had asked me questions about my flight and I only fed back small morsels of information, all false. Like a baffled princess, I had entered a kingdom of untruths, and this was now my plastic castle.

I told Miguel that my name was Vanessa and that I had been re-hired as an au pair for Julianne Moore, who was currently filming in the desert. The face of Miguel widened in amazement to hear of his new connection to Julianne Moore: through Vanessa, *his* passenger in *his* taxi. I told him that Julianne Moore had quite a temper, and when she wasn't scolding the children, she was scolding me. I conceived of a tragedy in which Julianne Moore had accidentally started a house fire, and I had saved the children, dragged them onto the garden lawn whilst her Beverly Hills mansion burned to the ground. But Julianne Moore had blamed me for the fire, until only this month, when she had seen sense and asked me to return to America.

Meek and humble, I told Miguel he could keep the change and watched the Toyota Prius dissolve inside the invisible heat, lost beneath the silver towers of the city that loomed in the distance like spacecrafts.

The heat was intense from the moment of stepping off the plane. At the airport, I unzipped my Hermès purse and could already feel the base of it stuck to my armpit. I rooted inside for the bottle of sparkling Pellegrino I had bought from the vending machine whilst waiting for Miguel's name to drift closer on the Uber app. An hour later and I was at the motel. My throat closed over as the receptionist approached, a small and business-like woman in a cheap blazer and stark *kabuki* makeup.

"Can I help you?" she asked, with a faint accent, possibly Canadian.

"Yes, hello. I know I haven't made a booking, but I was looking for a room, for possibly a few nights. Maybe... *five* nights?"

She smiled, the makeup creasing around her small mouth, as she turned to the computer screen and began to type on the keyboard. Behind her head was a calendar of a blank desert landscape. A fire ant scrambled from a single cracked tile along the wall, before sliding behind the shadow of the calendar.

"And your name?"

"Huh?" I replied, locked into the greasy elegance of the ant, its small body now drank inside the cool darkness.

"Your name. And identification."

"My name is Vanessa," I said. "Vanessa Harrington. I'm an au pair."

"I need identification for the booking."

I had to think quickly. I used my passport to enter the country but didn't want to reveal my movements any further. The front desk was peeling off in scabs of white paint. I glanced from the vase of dead sunflowers to the calendar on the wall and back to the receptionist. From the patio doors, I could hear the screams of children as they separated themselves from air and plunged into water, their bodies cleansed in powerful bleach. Above the liturgy of deck chairs and yellow parasols, a row of distressed palm trees fell apart across the smog-risen freeway.

"Well, that's just it… Charlie, is it?" I said, glancing down at the name badge pinned to her shirt. "I don't have any identification. I had it earlier at the airport, but it's been so terrible, Charlie. I must have had my passport stolen! I was buying a bottle of Pellegrino from the vending machine outside and turned only for a second. I will need to report it today. But first, I just need a room. I do have plenty of cash."

I then took the large bunch of American dollar bills from my purse, which I purchased at Gatwick. Delicately, I took five hundred-dollar bills and slid them across the desk.

"That can be for you, Charlie. For all your help on this matter. One for each night."

The girl looked down at the hundreds and then back at me.

Her face was pale and mottled beneath the chalky foundation. She had large dark nipples beneath the shirt. I thought of her undressing in the dank office behind the desk, her naked breasts running with fire ants, her mouth tucked into mine like a blood-burst poppy. An overhead fan beat air down onto the heads of us both, our scalps saturated with raw sweat, the weight of the loud air. I held my breath close inside my chest as a thin smile began to creep along the edges of her lips. A trembling crack revealed the acrylic teeth beneath. She turned back to the computer and continued typing. Slowly, she reached across, took the dollar bills, and folded them gently inside her pocket. "That's not a problem, Vanessa. Welcome to Sunset Creek."

7.

It was time to lay low. I stayed for three days and two nights in the motel room, plagued with flies squashed and spiralling through the air vents. The flies orbited around my head like winged satellites drunk on the sweat in my hair, my loud hormonal fear. Water was running from a patch of black damp leaking in the bathroom ceiling. In blackberry phalanxes, the flies fed on fatty pools of soap at the bottom of the oyster-pink bathtub. My pale wrists were covered in mosquito bites. They slept peacefully in the external wall inside slow vermillion nests.

On the third night, I crawled inside the bathtub,

and drank a cheap bottle of shiraz, and ordered room service. I dragged the television set from the bedroom and balanced it on the bathroom sink. I watched hours and hours of late-night shopping channels: Chinese imported jewellery, kaleidoscopic televangelists in purple vinyl suits selling the book of Deuteronomy, news broadcasts that induced a paranoid and endless American sleep. In a polite fashion, an Aryan blonde reporter confirmed the small beliefs of her viewers. Drowsily, I scrolled through article after article on my iPhone until suddenly, there it was.

A headline on the Guardian website.

FASHION PHOTOGRAPHER KILLED IN LONDON HOME.

There were pixels that made up her face. She was turned to the camera with a blank expression. It appeared anonymous, the distant look of someone you'd pass in the street. I almost didn't recognise her. My hands were shaking as I scrolled further.

CELINE STEIN, AGED 62, AN INTERNATIONALLY RESPECTED FASHION PHOTOGRAPHER THAT ROSE

TO FAME IN THE 1980S WORKING FOR CHANEL, WAS FOUND DEAD AT HER LONDON APARTMENT ON THURSDAY NIGHT BY FRIEND LUCÍA ESCARRA.

Trembling, the iPhone dropped from my hand onto the wet bathmat. I wiped away the remaining soap with a threadbare cotton towel. I put on a pair of Guess jeans and a plain green shirt before heading for the door.

At the end of the article was the simple statement.

INVESTIGATIONS ARE ONGOING. LONDON METROPOLITAN ARE ASKING FOR ANY INFORMATION ON THURSDAY NIGHT BETWEEN THE HOURS OF 11PM AND 1AM.

It was only a matter of time. I made the relevant phone call, and it was time to leave for the night. In my oversized sunglasses from the airport, I signalled for a taxi.

The desert wind blew warm carousels of rubbish around my high-heeled feet. The taxi was filled with cardboard Mexican saints glued to the insides of the doors. A small framed painting stood on the wooden dashboard. The image of a corpse. A bespectacled, elderly woman wrapped in bouquets of red carnations.

"Mama Lupita," said the driver, noticing me looking at the morbid image.

I smiled and nodded.

"You know her?" he asked.

"No. Is she your mother?"

The driver burst into a deep rumble of laughter from the bottom of his stomach. He didn't speak again as we moved deeper through the downtown area. The sky was turning purple above the spiked palm trees. The landscape here was a canvas of volcanic ash. Skeletons and fountains and buildings were lit up in magical fairy lights. The arcades of fluorescent strip clubs resembled Christmas grottoes. Cryogenic naked dancers glowed on their windowsills. Red alleyways led down into vacant parking lots. A shadow of an animal ran suddenly across a bare brick wall.

As we drove towards the steps of the Palazzo Resort, I handed the driver his money. He sealed it inside a small leather wallet in his blazer before tapping the photograph on the dashboard.

"A servant of God," he shouted as I staggered from the vehicle, turning to face the casino. Silently, he drove away.

As I made my way up the stone steps, I saw Celine slumped in the arms of her friend, unknown to me, Lucía Escarra. A beautiful and mysterious moment: Lucía finding Celine on her apartment floor and holding her as blood pooled down the arch of her neck, her pale shoulders sticky with plasma as the blood failed to clot. Tears were rolling down the sides of Lucía's cheeks like fruit unravelling.

Lighting a cigarette before entering the casino, I constructed an elaborate fantasy inside my mind, safely within the labyrinthine walls of the Alcazaba of Almería, where I had first met Celine. Beneath the Andalusian fortress, I built a medieval oubliette where my prisoners were thrown inside. They would never see the sun again. They would subsist on nothing but a handful of grain tossed inside a hole, sometimes a week at a time. Lucía and Celine. Their bodies were small and afraid.

The women huddled together for warmth during the winter months. They slowly learned the rhythm of each other's hearts. They knew that when the other's heart beat faster, there was a reason to be afraid. They began to fall in love with each other inside that sense of trepidation deep down beneath the earth. I saw the halogenic zombie of Mama Lupita rise from her grave, covered in electronic souvenirs and plastic lights. The soil around her headstone was bathed in the hot blood of goats she herded, the milk she fed back into peyote flowers. I invoked Mama Lupita as a hangman, an executioner holding a bucket of broken slate. Inside the dark oubliette, Mama Lupita shackled Celine and Lucía to the far wall. Scorched with the boiling midday sun, their breasts were bandaged and sealed beneath bloodied rags. With a silver mace, Mama Lupita's undead hand slashed their backs until they howled with tears. They wept with sorrow and pity for themselves. They wept because they had shared and understood the misery of the world. Their torture was an acceptance of a forbidden castle. She broke their arms across a felled log. She crushed their bodies with stones from a great height. The sky was like a purple carnival.

These towers rose up around me. Las Vegas was shaking with neon light, an oasis of pollution on the surface of a dark and unknowable moon. The fathomlessness of my husband's snoring suddenly came back to me, how he slept the entire night through his face. Eventually, I strapped an octopi machine to his mouth to quell the sound.

I never wanted this rage to go away. Celine, Lucía: they dissolved like witches inside carbon rising off green Mercedes outside the casino. A fluorescent vending machine stood alone as desert shadows elongated at dusk. I had created a cage from the bodies of zebras and licked the bars clean. My emaciated prisoners were led in elegant pools of zig-zagged blood. I decorated their corpses in the most beautiful flowers: slipper orchids and pink dahlias. Bald as geese, I tore every single hair from their screaming heads. An ark filled with red-clawed crabs. I drowned their lungs with the crimson fluid of my jealousy. Emperor scorpions, hummingbirds. Within me, there lived a kindness as bright and long as kitchen knives. I kissed her feet and forehead, her soft mouth. Above the body of Lucía, I scattered handfuls of chocolate cosmos.

8.

There's a silence in some men that I have always admired. I stand close to them and try to mimic their stillness, safe inside this radius of speechlessness. I imagine I am Frank Capra or Humphrey Bogart. I want the atomic zone of their silence to grow through my bones. A mute shadow lost in blue cigarette smoke. There is a concealment to the mute person. He looks into your wide eyes, but his lips remain closed. He carries a paradox inside his larynx. He holds a locket inside his mouth. I was like a beautiful boy covered in black lilies, waiting inside an office of maniacs. The men blew nicotine into my face. Their boss sat across from me. He carried within himself that same reassuring silence I was certain moved through his entire skeleton.

"Thank you for seeing me, Mr Garcia."

His wrists were branded with scribblings, cuboid doves—green and illegible tattoos. He wore a starched shirt with not a single crease. His immaculate clothing was met with an incongruous, toadlike head. It peered upward from the column of clean fabric. Above his lip ran a bed of white hair, a powerful moustache on his tanned face. I sat still in the chair, keeping my eyes on the mahogany desk and the tapestry of grooves knifed into the dark wood. His associate stood at the door of the office in a pale Armani suit with a black handgun in a holster visible at the hip. At the opposite end of the room were two men smoking cigarettes and watching episodes of *Curb Your Enthusiasm* on a small television plugged into the wall.

"Do you like?" asked the associate at the door, frowning as he looked across at the men enthralled in their show.

"Huh?" I asked, unsure of the question. "*Curb Your Enthusiasm?*"

"Do you like the show?" he asked, again. His face was fluent and open.

"Larry David, right?"

"Yeah, Larry David."

We remained in silence for a few more minutes whilst Mr Garcia went into an adjacent office. Occasionally, the associates glanced at my face and legs, my breasts tucked into the oversized bra.

The adjoining offices were located at the back of the casino through a small blue corridor. A strip of white paint ran horizontally along the centre of the wall, moving from doorframe to doorframe. There must have been at least fifty doors, each painted black with large brass numbers nailed to them. The casino rented the rooms out to a handful of independent businesses. It has not been hard to find the details of their services online. I sent them an email, and within ten minutes, I received a reply with a set of questions then another with a list of instructions. I made sure to bring my passport and driving license, checking again as I climbed inside the sweltering taxi. The highway was filled with piles of hot garbage that flung themselves north-east towards the desert, green plastic Sprite bottles roaming free and wild like berserk orphans. Plastic lost in endlessness, a crystalline pink dusk. I thought of farmhands out there in the darkness, working dawn to sundown in squalid stables, their rancid blood swelling and mixing in the air with the hatred of the horses they tended, channelling their cruel slavery of animals back into the earth, golden spears of wheat.

When I was a child, my mother (a trembling alcoholic) had given me a sheet of paper and a crayon. And on the page, I drew a figure with a single line. A horse made of blue wax. I had never seen a horse before, but somehow, there it was. I had conjured the beast from my imagination. Within seconds, my mother tore the drawing to shreds. It had awakened a horrible fear in her and we never spoke of the horse again.

"Mr Garcia will be with you again in a few moments."

A polite name for a sensible man. A man with etiquette and the time and resources to help others in need. He entered once again and sat across from me.

"Passport and driving license, please. And we will need the $5,000 now."

I took out the huge stack of bills from my purse. The majority of the notes had been inside the lining of the suitcase. I had taken more in the last few weeks from the children's savings account. The keypad of the machine in London had a yellow arrow and a green tick. Actions become nothing but movement and rhythm as I pressed down on the metal language. A flow chart, chalk hopscotch washed away in the rain.

When they children had been small, their bodies had always felt cold and heavy against my own. Holding them offered a sense of gravity similar to inserting smooth pebbles inside your pocket. I fell pregnant at the age of thirty-three. Like an obscene satellite, I was dragged out of my carefree orbit. And soon, I began to sink closer to Earth. I was a UFO. The weight of my own bowels were filled with the flesh of impossible things. Pregnancy was like one of those exhibitions at the science museum, where you see Neanderthals sinking into enormous pits of tar, their primitive eyes not understanding the logic of their own extinction. Maps showing continents devouring each other to make room for more complex evils, an industrialised psychosis.

In those first years, when the children drank my milk and ate bits of my hair, swallowed my *fingernails* in their mouth, I was shocked and saddened. It felt like cannibalism. I could see the hunger in their flashing eyes and impish faces. Like proboscis monkeys, they pressed their bulbous heads into the bars of the cot. Starved gibbons that tore at my blouse and skin. I felt abandoned in those infancy years, absent and alone, lost in some Malaysian sorrow. I wandered through a death-dream like the sparkling aisles in a Bukit Bintang shopping mall. I was filled with a bloodborne tropical disease.

"I want my new name on each identification to be Vanessa," I said to the associate and then louder for his boss to hear, "Vanessa *Harrington*."

"It means nothing to us," said the associate flatly, as he returned a few minutes later with a sealed envelope that he handed to one of the other men. I continued looking at the wall behind the head of Mr Garcia, until finally, I returned to his blank and ambivalent expression. He was staring directly into my eyes. Beneath the moustache of white hair, his mouth began to open. His voice was clear and elegant.

"And what are you running from, Vanessa?"

I smiled, nervously. I didn't expect any questions once I had showed the money. I steadied my hands and folded them together underneath the table. "Nothing," I replied, calmly. "I just need a change."

Mr Garcia smiled, his eyes lightening for a moment.

"That is the correct answer."

And with that, he asked me to sit at the far side of the room, opposite the television. He took an iPhone from his blazer pocket and asked me to look forward. I stared back at his face, covered partially now as he glanced down at my image on the screen. He snapped about five times.

"Reborn, like Lazarus himself," he said on the final flash, grinning widely. His mouth was filled with false gold teeth.

I left the office with the new driving license and passport. The corridor remained empty. I peered at the pale image on the passport, looking back beneath the iridescent hologram, conjured from the blank photocopier. I placed the documents inside my pocket. I could hear a key turn behind me. The number nailed to the door was 38.

9.

Slow breath left their frail and elderly bodies. Weakly, they stood in front of fruit machines, enacting the repetition of towers covered in serpentine dragons. Jealous leprechauns, cowboys erupting into silver coins. A rich, deep carpet ebbed outwards from their sandalled feet in psychedelic and insane shapes toward the darkest corner of the casino where a large plastic hut stood. A man was handing out yellow tokens from a window to the gathering patrons. It was happy hour, and the tokens were cheaper to buy. The figures stood still around the roulette, and their shadows darkened with each seizure of light as the wheel turned loudly, offering each soul a carnival of hieroglyphics: a purple plum, a yellow banana, the number 777. Their red-soaked eyeballs with vodka-expanded capillaries, blinked rapidly beneath pillars of argon-generated lamps. Each processed and understood the language of the casino like Mesoamerican script. They lifted their arms. I watched skeletons turn ultraviolet inside the shock of each win. It was like being hit by lightning.

Sealing my purse, I walked past the roulette wheel that began to accelerate again at the touch of a gloved hand. I needed another drink or some food. The white ball hopped between the red and black zones of the circle—its frenzied, schizoid face. The croupier waited in an absent tuxedo. His pale eyes looked over the expectations of his generous amphitheatre, men and women that rested gigantic cocktail glasses on the faux Roman décor, jugs of oily piña coladas resting on a polystyrene alcove modelled on the Pantheon.

"A hamburger with fries," I said, as I reached the bar in the corner and scanned the menu quickly. I could sense the server looking down at my skirt.

"Do you have a drink voucher? You can get a

glass of white wine with that for free."

Brusquely, I told him I didn't. He shrugged and poured me a glass anyway. The man was short and Italian. He told me his name was Flavio. He asked me a series of questions that I avoided. I made it clear I was more interested in eating my hamburger and looking through Instagram.

When Mr Garcia had taken my photograph that evening, I was filled with a sense of desertion. There is an emptiness to having your photo taken that is akin to time reversing. It was always the same. Being photographed means falling out of time. As a child, I found being photographed terrifying. My father had left when I was six years old and for the rest of my upbringing, I became as transparent as an eel. I was convinced I could pour milk through my own hand. I would hold the carton above my forearm and watch milk pass right through the flesh. When my mother beat me, she would always make *me* apologise afterwards. For making *her* so angry and making her do it. There were nights when I prayed for magical powers. I saw constellations of distant green stars that moved through the hem of my school shirt. I read comic books at lunchtime, hidden away in the corner of the break room or the outskirts of the playground. Soon, I became convinced that I harboured the same catastrophic power as Doctor Manhattan. If I opened my palm to the school wall, then the whole of New York City would fold inside my palm like a piece of origami.

I dreamed all day long of hurting my mother. I ran through raspberry brambles until my face tore into scalding patches of blood. The blood mingled with the taste of autumnal fruit into new and wild cordials. Staring at kitchen knives hanging from their magnetic kitchen rack, I imagined I was a Russian princess that harboured telekinesis. I could speak with aliens from a blue and imaginary planet. I escaped from home. It all happened so quickly, a few years in the blink of an eye. I went to my first modelling photoshoot in Mayfair. Trembling, I took off my clothes and put on a creased piece of lingerie. It hadn't been changed since the previous model. Her sweat pressed into my skin. Her dreams were carelessly flung across my shoulders. I carried the heavy burden of her dreams with me into the room like a broken hunchback. When the camera flashed, I was bombarded with the same radiation as Doctor Manhattan locked inside his test chamber. I rose into the air like an ultraviolet flame. Holding the nothingness of a mirror, I saw a deep and endless silence as wide as night falling through my hair. My mouth opened and closed in front of the photographer like a puzzled machine. He smiled, and I turned like a frozen rook towards the king. His photograph captured the same as Mr Garcia: nothingness, a chimera harbouring the sacred power of invisibility. I met the supernatural shiver of light across my skin, the equinox of my own poisoned blood. Moonlit jellyfish in Miami, crocodiles swimming in bright charcoal water, the blankness of electricity moving through a socket. "Have another one." Flavio said, as he pushed the beer glass towards me.

Taking out the large stack of bank notes, I paid Flavio for the meal. The casino became louder. The machines began to ring in unison. Totems of neon flushed and swam towards the ceiling like red pterodactyls. Currency flowed through their insides. Hot pink enemas inside lime green slots. A frenzied flamenco feeding of fantasies and hope.

The veins in the hamburger oozed with clear fat as I pushed down on the remaining part of the soft bread. Turning back to Flavio, I suddenly heard a couple arguing at the other side of the bar. The man was stocky and attractive, with a big bulldog face. He was bald with large arms covered in tattoos. As he spoke, he spilled a pitcher of beer down his T-shirt.

"Fuck you," he shouted, putting the pitcher back on the bar. "Stupid fucking whore."

She went to hit him, but he grabbed her arm. I could only see her from the back, but I could tell her body was shaking. She was much smaller than him. Her hair was platinum blonde. As he held her wrist, she managed to twist herself round like a wind-up doll. The room span around her. A ballerina inside a snow globe. It was then I saw her face smeared with makeup. Her eyes were stinging with tears. She looked exactly like Celine.

My heart stopped. Her expression was almost identical, even how the bottom lip hung open before she started to cry. The same ovoid eyes. Dumbfounded, I dropped my fork and heard it clatter loudly on the plate. The man threw her arm to one side and stormed to the opposite side of the casino. He pushed open the exit doors with his huge fists. A security guard followed him outside. The girl, defeated, let out a weak sob and fell to the floor.

10.

On the brightest day of spring, the photograph of Celine creased in my hands. I held it, trembling like a mirage inside the endless afternoon pouring through the windows of the house. Somehow, it had folded to meet the shape of the wall, the gradual geometries of months and years. It had softened with the heat of those years as it pressed itself between the skirting board and the dressing table. My perfume bottles lay as spotless as immaculate crystals lined up in the bright, singing light. But when you lifted one of the bottles up, you saw a faint circle of grey-lilac dust. You could smell their cruel insides: ylang-ylang, cypress, ambergris. The nightmare wax of whales wiped down your bare breasts. I unscrewed all of the bottles, and the clouds in the bedroom window flung themselves across the cathedral blue sky.

Naked, I wanted to paint a reflection of myself on the surface of the mirror that reflected nothing back but the empty room. Often, I would play a game where I almost left the bedroom and looked back from the doorway. I could see the deserted space from a diagonal angle in the mirror. The king-sized bed, the pine table, the wardrobe door slightly ajar, stacked full of his office shirts. It was like seeing the invisible game played by furniture, a silent joke that only they understood. The mockery of a single chair, alone in the centre of the house.

It had been the brightest day of spring when I decided to clean the room. I could see the dust everywhere. I lifted up the base of the chair and the runner around the bed. Finally, the dressing table, only to find the crumpled photograph of Celine beneath. She had been sleeping next to me all this time, nestled inside that dark space. Her face was a web of creases, a tarantula lost inside a labyrinth. She was stood in front of a large expanse of water. I remembered our trip to Windermere in the Lake District.

The light was trembling across my hand. When I looked at the mirror, there was no reflection. I saw the true emptiness of mirrors, the expanse of their silver weariness. The silent glass sang of a loneliness of the room and the silver-grey undersides of clouds. Every mirror in the house fell silent beneath a sheet of darkness as I wandered towards the window where the photograph formed an eclipse between myself and the dressing table. The photograph had thinned and I could see my hand swimming behind the paper like a goblin shark moving beneath the shape of Celine. She was smiling.

And here she was again. Somehow, in the Las Vegas casino. The stranger was supine on the carpet, writhing at my feet like a medieval slave. Her head hung low, but I recognised the same small bridge of the nose. The way she carried herself strongly like an acrobat, as though an invisible string pulled her upwards from the solar plexus.

I reached down to help the crying girl, but she pushed me away. She didn't need me. The security guard, who was looking around concerned, returned to his post by the door.

"Give me a beer," she said to Flavio, flinging her purse aggressively onto the bar, a few seats down from where I had been eating. Flavio pushed a cold bottle of Budweiser towards her. She drank in long gulps, gasping as she wiped her face. Her mascara was black and runny on the back of her hand. She ordered another beer and placed some dollar bills on the bar. Flavio took them and went about his business serving the other customers.

"Do you want some?" I asked, signalling to the bowl of fries that came with the hamburger.

The girl looked at me suspiciously, her small face wrinkled up. I could see a remaining flash of anger in her eyes, the aftershock of adrenaline running through her body.

"I don't need no charity, lady." Her accent was southern. I smiled and pushed the bowl towards her.

"They will only go to waste."

She scowled, but without saying anything, she began to eat from the bowl. She had a tattoo on the inside of her left wrist of a four-leaf clover.

She looked thinner than Celine, but her face was identical. It didn't take long for her to consume the food. She continued to drink her bottle of beer. Turning from me, she began to fumble through her purse. I could see her eyes were still brimming with tears. She looked exhausted.
"Who was that guy?"

She swivelled quickly towards me. "Why *the fuck* do you care, lady? Huh?" she asked, exasperated. I didn't respond. She continued to look inside her purse with jabbing actions like a mole furrowing through a patch of dirt. Surprisingly, she started to speak. "Just another fuckhead. My husband-to-be. He drinks a few beers and thinks he's fucking Vin Diesel. You know the type?" I nodded. "We're here to watch the wrestling. Dwayne Johnson? The Rock?"

I nodded again.

"I'm sorry, lady. I just," her eyes were shining as she tried to reapply some mascara, "I'm just... I'm just having a rough day. I thought maybe we were coming here to get married. You know, like a surprise. But I genuinely think he just wants to go see The Rock." She began to laugh to herself before finishing the last of the beer and holding her hand out to me. "My name is Kaylee. We came up from Memphis."

I took her small hand and shook it. She had on a silver bracelet that shimmied in the lights above the bar.

"I'm Vanessa."

"You're British, right? I can tell from the accent. I'm real good at accents. I just heard one in the bar the other day. From *Birmingham*, over there. Ryan, he loves this show called *Peaky Blinders*. He loves anything with Tom Hardy in."

She smiled and looked down again. She seemed a little embarrassed. I was deeply attracted to her. The jarring sounds of the casino had formed a continuous drone in the background: an ambient wasteland of promised wealth inside golden atriums where men and women pressed at humming buttons inside the cacophony of gratified machines. Her platinum hair was swimming in the chandeliers hung from the ceiling. Her pink nipples were visible beneath the white cotton shirt.

"And what do you do, Vanessa? For work." she asked, drawing me back to her pale grey-green eyes.

"I work for Julianne Moore," I answered, signalling for Flavio to send over two more beers. Kaylee's mouth dropped open as she burst out laughing.

"That's fucking insane, like literally insane," she replied, holding the cold beer up as to toast me.

"Like what, as her personal assistant?"

"I'm her agent. I organise roles for her in film and television and stuff."

'Wow, that's so cool! She was in *The Hunger Games*, right? And that old one with the ten-pin bowling?"

"*The Big Lebowski*, yes. She's a big deal."

"You must know lots of people in Hollywood then," she said, smiling as she swigged the last of the beer.

"We don't have many celebrities down in Memphis. They're bringing the *Real Housewives* franchise to the city, though. For Bravo. You ever watch it?"

I nodded. She burst out laughing again.

"Those bitches are fucking whack-jobs. Ryan loves it too. He pretends not to watch it when I have it on. I think he would fuck any of those wives. He loves bimbos with big tits."

I smiled and finished my beer. Kaylee began to rifle through her purse again.

"Were you about to hit him before?"

A look of suspicion flashed again across her face. Her hands were still inside the purse when her back arched. Her body had the chronology of an animal cornered. She hunched over like when a creature folds into itself to protect its internal organs. I was worried I had asked too much. She didn't answer the question.

"The fucker took my cigarettes *and* my fucking lighter. Look, Vanessa. I need to get out here and find a smoke. Do you want to take a walk?"

I shrugged and nodded. We left by the fire exit. The sun had started to slip across the horizon in orange waves of light. The streets were lit up in rows of neon arcades. Bodegas lost in blue mucus and insect song. We found a small kiosk, and she paid for a packet of Marlboros and a small Bic lighter. She lit the cigarette and inhaled deeply. I could smell the sweat on her body in the sweet summer night. The end of the cigarette glowed with each breath, following the bright pulse of each new moment. She took out a small glass bottle and sprayed herself in perfume. Later, she told me it was her favourite. Midnight by Britney Spears.

11.

Her small feet were hung from the end of the bed at Sunset Creek. The nails were painted in cobalt polish. She had removed her tights which lay crumpled and serpentine in the corner. Like Celine, Kaylee spoke with a calm voice. She generated a certain authority in her confidence and effortless sexuality. She looked exactly like Celine except for the big platinum blonde hair. I wondered if she had fake tits. I could tell she found me beautiful. She was in the presence of a rare carnivorous flower, a lime green flytrap. I was like an exotic alien to her Yankee brain. I kept looking at the inside of her mouth, at the yellow unwashed teeth. In the time it had taken to pour out the miniature bottles of wine from the fridge, she had thrown her jacket to the opposite side of the room and slipped off her stilettos. I watched them fall from her toes in the twinkling light.

She apologised for the smell of her feet, which I pretended not to notice—a thick and earthy smell, like handfuls of wet sand. My hand began to tremble as I thought of the body of Celine sinking backwards through its own liquorice fluid pouring from the diaphragm split apart like a blood-black tambourine. I fell into another daydream where I was like the shadow of some monstrous puppet. It was midnight in Almería. I came across a silent graveyard filled with sun-bleached tombstones and brushed my hands across ceramic urns and pots. A single red carnation. In the daydream, I was like a blue djinn. Rising from a fountain in the centre of a courtyard, I was an assassin levitating above a shining minaret. A bullet moved vertically through the face of Celine, rupturing into bone and noise. "Is that the bathroom?" Kaylee asked, pointing to the door in the wall.

I nodded solemnly and placed both wine glasses on the shelf above the bed. We had wandered from bar to bar, getting more and more inebriated. We ordered margheritas haloed in broken frosted salt. Each glass was bisected with large slices of sour lime.

At the bar, Kaylee told me she was a Virgo and how that made her selfish and sarcastic. She told me about her father who had died of an uncurable form of cancer. Many years ago, he had worked in factory in Memphis that manufactured stoves where he welded the parts together. Unknown to him and his co-workers, they were breathing in asbestos every day. The asbestos took twenty-three years to reveal itself. It sat dormant inside her father's lungs until one day, sensing some shift in the atmosphere, it began to crystalise in his dark interior. It slowly murdered her silent and unknowable father in a matter of months. Never telling a soul, he dropped dead one day outside a postal office. She had met Ryan not soon afterwards. He was working as a sports physiotherapist but following a night of heavy drinking, he was served with a DUI, and his employer let him go.

"There's the life you imagine and then the life you get given. People speak about ambition like it's an option for most people, but it's just a myth sold by people with big houses and loving families.

Ambition has fucking nothing to do with anything," Kaylee sneered as she drunkenly motioned to the empty faces in the bar. "When I was a little girl, I used to watch Judy Garland in *A Star is Born* all the time. She was my favourite. And there's trolley scene from *Meet Me in St. Louis*, you know it?"

I nodded, smiling.

"Judy was something," she continued. "I'd spent all my days acting out those scenes. Imaginary scenes from a future life. I'd play music and pretend I was in a film and do awful acts like killing an enemy. What it would be like to rob a bank, you know? Or I'd pretend the phone just rang, and it was the police saying my husband had drowned off the coast of Peru. Stupid shit like that."

"It's fun to pretend."

"It is fun!" she exclaimed, her face shining with relief, signalling for the waiter to bring more shots. "Like if were in a film now, maybe you would tell me a secret?"

"What kind of secret?"

"Something bad, something *heart-breaking*. And I'd swear not to tell a single soul. And to prove it, I'd tell you something back."

"I don't have any secrets, Kaylee."

"Bullshit."

I could tell she was completely wasted from the way she was slurring her words. Her aggressive manner had softened into a strange intimacy. She saw me as a companion, an ally in a world with odds stacked against us. I wanted to reach across and kiss her.

"OK. I'm not really Julianne Moore's agent."

Her eyes widened, and she burst into loud laughter.

"I fucking knew it! You're far too pretty to be someone's agent. I bet you're an actress too, yes? You lying bitch."

"I do work for Julianne Moore, but I'm her au pair. I look after her kids."

Kaylee continued laughing, taking the fresh tequila shots and pouring one into each of our margherita glasses.

"An au pair? That's not as glamorous as an agent. But still, do you think I could meet her? Maybe, you know, I could move to California."

She spoke about wanting to be an actress as a child after her mother showed her Veronica Lake in *I Married a Witch*. Her favourite holiday was Halloween. Ryan had asked her to move in with him when they were on holiday in Miami. She later found out it was because he was broke. She showed me photographs on her phone of them beside a pool filled with inflatable dolphins and leathery elderly faces. The bar was closing. Kaylee suggested coming back to my motel because she didn't want to see Ryan whilst he was still angry. I felt close to her and, by extension, to Celine. I kept looking at her face. It was like watching a hologram projected onto the surface of a mannequin. On the silver bracelet on her wrist, I noticed small blue daisies. Drunkenly, she told me about the orbit of Mercury and made links to the antidepressant she was taking. She confided in me about the lack of sex in her relationship, how he jerked off to cartoonish pornography of women with silicone tits that spoke in infantile gobbledegook, whilst she'd been having an on-off affair with an acquaintance she actually despised.

When we arrived back at the motel, I was surprised to find the pool had been completely drained. Me and Kaylee stood at the edge of the cavernous pit. The desert wind blew warm air into our faces. Sat on the bed afterwards, I could hear her pissing loudly in the bathroom. Quickly, I took the stacks of dollar bills from my handbag and the rest from beneath the mattress, and put them all in the safe in the wall. I heard the shower quickly come on, and a few minutes later, Kaylee opened the door. She was completely naked, pressing a fresh towel across her breasts and stomach. "What now?" she asked.

She moved to the bed and let the towel drop. We began to kiss, and then as she lay down, I put my tongue up her ass. She was writhing on the bed. I put my fingers down her throat, and her eyes began to brim with tears. In the filthy room, she crawled towards me like a dog. With one hand, I took her hair, and with the other I pressed my fingers again inside her. She was making a low begging sound. I could feel her coming around my hand, and then I could smell her cunt and ass. I sucked on her tits as she lay spiralling through the sheets of the bedding, weeping like a carousel of pain and loneliness. Her face and ass cheeks were streaked with sweat, and the torn sachets of lube I used to plunge half my fist up her. We drowned in the sound of traffic-choked on its own pollution, heading south into downtown. Exhausted at dawn, our heads crashed through each other. Lapping at my clit, I held her head very still between my legs. Closing my eyes, all I could hear was the air conditioning that maintained the delicate homeostasis of the room. I unclenched my thighs and guided her face deeper into my hole. Struggling, she began to jut out her jaw, which made me come harder. I wanted our skeletons to break each other. Her stupid little pink pussy. Her smooth brown asshole. I gave her the nightmare she wanted, fed it back through her small mouth. I was the destroyer from Mars.

12.

The morning had been warm and uncomfortable. It lingered and stretched itself across the damp walls of the badly ventilated room. The alcohol was still thudding on the inside of my skull, blood pulsing through the wrists. I had felt the surface of her thin body stick to mine throughout the night. She smelled faintly of vomit at one point. I could sense her presence in the bathroom when she staggered up to go and piss again. Her feet slapped loudly against cold marble. Throughout the night, I was plagued with dreams of Celine. I accepted these dreams and the dread they brought. It was like making a pact with an illness. I accepted and went to bed, knowing I would sink inside this dreadful feeling.

With Kaylee next to me, I had dreamed that Celine had been vacuum-packed and sealed inside a laundry bag. I was at an international airport, possibly Rome, waiting for a plane. When suddenly, along the conveyor belt, the corpse of Celine was rotating with all the other suitcases. Her face was pressed up close like a creased animal. Stood amongst the other tourists, I pretended not to notice. None of the other people stood about seemed to care and resumed with their conversations. Her breath was condensing on the inside of the bag.

Startled, I awoke a few times. The cool and caramel shoulder of Kaylee calmed me down. At one point, she rolled over, and I could feel her hands reach out and rest on the inside of my lower stomach. Naked, the air ventilator finally poured a cold channel of air through a grid in the wall, a stainless-steel corridor that snaked the entire motel. I had noticed a map of the ventilation system on the wall behind the main door. Insects chirped loudly and crawled up and down the long patio doors that opened onto the balcony. The insects were singing to the empty nocturnal desert, a lunar zone of abandoned villas, *departamentos* built from hot Carson City brick.

In the morning, after she cleaned herself a little, we spoke for over two hours. She told me about her earlier life and how she had fallen pregnant to Ryan but lost the baby four months later.

"We didn't really speak about it afterwards. He put all his energy into wrestling, you know? He was obsessed at that point with Triple H," she said, flicking her cigarette into the black plastic tray provided beside the television. I pretended to know what she was talking about. "I think he could have made a pretty good father, but not now."

Pulling her towards me, she let her shirt fall away. On the inside of her thigh was a tattoo of a falling star. On her shoulder, she had the word PETER inked in small illegible font. I found them both ugly but smiled when she explained them. "Embarrassing, right?" she giggled. I shook my head to reassure. "He was my brother. He died in Afghanistan. He *really* didn't like Ryan."

When she laughed, a pair of small wrinkles

formed equally on both sides of her mouth. She must have had lip fillers in the last few weeks as they had that sore, glossy look. Beneath her shoulders, her skin was slightly mottled with tanning lotion. She told me that she had never been with a woman before.

"Do you know many dykes?" she asked, half-smiling in the sheltered light coming in through the patio windows.

I laughed and nodded. I lied. I didn't know any dykes. I had seen them every day on public transport in London, in skinhead drag with Fred Perry polos and fashionable short haircuts. I carried these judgements inside myself like bits of broken glass.

Kaylee spoke about us going for breakfast together and escaping the humid room. My head was still hurting from the alcohol last night. Outside, the world resembled a painfully bright and lawless realm. I could feel another migraine coming. It ran from the vertex of my skull sharply down through my entire shattered face. The colours in the room had begun to throb in shining, painful sequences. It hurt even to look at Kaylee now, so I

turned to lie down and sleep once more.
"We should get out of here, there's a great café downtown?" she pursued again.

I shook my head because the pain was now unbearable. I could see the naked shape of Kaylee, her silhouette framed against the pale, ambiguous sky. Drifting through the window came the incessant screams of children from the swimming pool.

"Could you lend me any money for a taxi home?" I finally heard her ask.

Immobile, I closed my eyes and must have slept for the remainder of the afternoon. I dreamed of Kaylee but now she was Celine. Her arms encased me. Numbness ran backwards through the motel room. The moon hung above us both, lost beneath a filigree and lilac desert. Her voice was calm as it passed through the sleeping bodies of coyotes. A faceless man stood in an empty canteen serving ladles of chilli into ceramic bowls. He ate maize chips from a filth-ridden tray. Aloe plants folded over the naked thighs of Kaylee in soft, streaked moisture, her open mouth like a silver bathroom faucet. I tried to summon myself out of these dreams into the waking, monotonous motel room. I was inside the lobby filled with photographs of endless highways. A desert rancho engulfed in black night. I slid a gigantic sawed-off shotgun into my own mouth and looked up. The wall above the bed was like an endless waterfall. My body was a red scarecrow. I had projected myself into the motel television and sat down before my mother. She was drunk and screaming on the screen. She had torn out all of her own hair. This was all a migraine hallucination. Celine, pristine and perfect, passed a microphone back and forth and asked a series of garbled questions.

"Do you know this person?" Celine mouthed, and held up a photograph on the screen. It was a photograph of herself.

Celine had taken many self-portraits in her career. She had a period in Leipzig where she destroyed her entire apartment and took photos of herself and friends living in the ruins of the building. On the photograph, she was stood at an empty kitchen counter. The light was streaming through the inside of her arm as she lifted a cup of coffee to her mouth. You could see the contents of the cup. A dark and viscous fluid. There were lumps of grey rubble around her feet. The profile of her face was sharp and striking, her expression vaguely distant as though trying to remember a person she knew a long time ago from another place.

In my dreams, I always saw hell as a faraway land populated with rare and exquisite birds. I tied myself up in beautiful zirconium chains. Inside the centre of the migraine, I punished myself in the hurricane of my own mind. Thunderstorms rolled across the desert plains. A bolt of frightened lightning moved through the body of a coatimundi.

My daughter suddenly appeared on the television. Her body had been badly burned in a terrible fire. On the screen, she resembled something inhuman: a melted chicken or a small bird-like dinosaur.

Waking suddenly from the migraine, I found a note from Kaylee tucked under the pillow next to mine. 7TH & CARSON CAFÉ. TOMORROW. 12PM NOON.

13.

The migraine continued to envelope me in its own immediacy, like an entrance into a close and solitary space. Wandering out of the motel room, I made my way past the reception desk, where Charlie stood in the same shirt, staring down as she filed away at her large acrylic nails. She held a French tip close to her pockmarked face and blew clumsily. She, along with all the children running around the pool, resembled shapes belonging to another destiny. People have cancers growing inside them because their body is following a unique route from life towards death. Electricity spiralled through endless telegraph poles from Sunset Creek into the north and infinite desert. A beehive of helicopters levitated above a single cabin where a man cooked meth inside a concrete hole. Green aloe ejaculated across the backs of blind ants.

I wanted nothing from these other guests as I walked towards the vending machine in the far corner of the courtyard and pressed for a cold can of 7UP and a bag of salted chips. My exhaustion revealed the failure of every person I encountered. The pittance they dressed up as humility, the herd they had hypnotised into becoming a family. It was a relief to need nothing from humanity. My divorce from the population was as obvious as a housefly landing on a Thanksgiving turkey. I crawled across this planet. I wandered back across the courtyard and went to look at the empty pool on the outskirts of the motel lot, tucked away behind a wire fence. Me and Kaylee must have walked that way back from the taxi but I was unable to recall. We thought the main pool had been drained, drunkenly. It was clear now there was a second pool, empty and derelict, behind the motel.

"I've never been with a woman before," Kaylee confessed to me, as we folded into each other like red shadows, her ass spread apart on the clean white linen. She told me she had an alcoholic mother that beat her, too. She told me she had a twin sister that died in childbirth, and her mother blamed her for the murder. Being born had been a crime smeared down the face of the silent babe.

I was making my way to my room, through the lobby, when suddenly Charlie rose from her chair with a look of determination glowing softly in her cherubim face.

"Mrs Harrington," she smiled, "How are you finding your stay at Sunset Creek?"

I could see how large her nipples were through the pale shirt.

"Very well, thank you, Charlie," I mumbled, my head still hurting and feeling unable to speak, navigating the odd moments of clarity that the migraine afforded suddenly like coming up for air.

"That's wonderful, Mrs *Harrington*," stressing the last part in a playful kind of mockery, "It's just that we will really need to see some identification."

I stared back at her, unblinking.

"It had been two days now, and it is hotel policy," she said.

Her face was shining in the light of the reception as the bright glare of the pool reflected off the patio doors. I could hear the soft extractor fan behind her head as it sucked out warm moisture and replaced it with a frozen shaft of artificial air. Sweat had formed in soft petals around the collar of her shirt. Her smile began to crease again at the ends of her mouth. Fumbling inside my pocket, I brought out the laminated identification that Mr Garcia had printed in the office space at the casino and rested it on the marble reception desk. Charlie's hand snatched up the card with her crab-like nails. She held it close to the computer screen as she sullenly filled in the new details. I could see the rainbow hologram flickering across the surface of my photograph. My face drenched in ultraviolet grease.

Towards the end of the affair, when Celine took my picture, it felt like an x-ray. I was certain she could see my insides, my intestines loaded with jealousy like long and ornate serpents, a tapeworm wrapped through the machinery of the camera as she told me to take off my sports bra in her

Highgate apartment. Celine had been married at the time, to one of her many girlfriends. The girl had died in a car crash in Milan, gone straight through the windscreen.

At the time, I believed it was my hatred that forbid her from putting on the seatbelt that February morning. I was a powerful witch descending on Italy. My jealousy had built up inside the car like a fog beneath her seat and shoved her face-first, a rocket into the glass.

Envy is a compass that leads one to far and distant planets. It allows one to conquer many worlds. I looked at the corpse of Celine spinning beneath black Uranian swamps and it was all mine to claim. Like medieval hounds or a triplet of Furies (myself, my hatred, my jealousy), we feasted as victorious as cannibals on the corpse of Celine. I dreamed of her floating in the centre of the motel pool in a bright field of opulent blue. Her skin had started to bleach and rot beneath the Marc Jacobs sunglasses—a necromancer in a powder pink bikini. Light streamed through a golden sarcophagus buried in the centre of the Mojave Desert. I needed to see her again. I needed to see Kaylee.

"That all looks OK," said Charlie, handing back the fake identification.

The misery in her face was blatant. She had wanted to extort more money out of me for her own secret aims. She had wanted to conquer this miserable place. In the end, we're all the same.

14.

Maximum Platinum read the cursive font on the small pot of hairy dye. There were two sections to the pot, which unscrewed from each end. One contained a thick violet paste, and the other was bright yellow. I dragged the mirror from the far wall into the centre of the room inside a spiralling hive of dust that circled above the glass in a broken snowstorm. The entire motel was infested. I could hear the wasps growing fat under my bed. As I yanked out the hairdryer cable from the plug socket, a pink cloud of desiccated ants swam through the air around my face and shoulders. Before blow drying, I sealed the hair down with consecutive strips of aluminium foil. The metal glowed white beneath the heat.

I had dyed my hair many times before, in rooms alone or with other models, often the night before a photoshoot. One night in Tokyo, I had to walk for two hours to find some red dye. There was a small cabin at the side of the road. It was pouring with rain. Inside the cabin was a small man surrounded by towers of soaked newspapers that he had dragged inside from the street. Above his head, from a metal link chain, hung a cage. Inside was a live lobster. Its round body stood closely to the lightbulb swinging against the front of the cage, which refracted shadows across its dark maroon shell that encased the head. Its red claws were tied in string.

"He's asleep," said the shopkeeper in clear and impressive English. I then noticed the cosmetics behind his head—small boxes of hair dye. There was a brand of red dye called BAMBOO ARMAGEDDON. The packet showed a strange drawing of a panda bear on fire. The lobster remained still in its cage as I signalled and paid for the product.

Earlier that morning, I saw the Guardian

and a number of other news outlets had updated their report about Celine's murder. The floor gave way beneath me. I was existing inside a vague simulation close to sleep. In dreams now, I crawled towards the lobster. I was living inside the red desert of its mind. Comatose, there were insects asleep at the base of the empty swimming pool next to Sunset Creek. Beneath daytime moons, the insects opened their blank wings.

Reading the article about twelve times, I wanted to vomit eventually and dived towards the toilet bowl. *How long would it take for the gun to shore up?* I wanted these migraines to never go away because they connected me to her like an iron chain on a shipwrecked boat. I dreamed of black waters running backwards and forwards through a plasma television, her face with its eyeballs and tongue removed. Upon a vast surgical table lay the supine body of Kaylee. Her face was riddled with red mosquitos bites. Her forehead and mouth were bloated. A Persian curse was whispered into her ear, and suddenly, her eyes flung wide open. She was under the trance of a mummy, secret purple flowers that lined the banks of the Nile. I swam through the heat of the Nevada desert to find her beautiful body unwrapped.

Trembling, later that morning, I scrolled again down to the Guardian article on my phone to read there was further information to all the articles. There was an image of my face with some text beneath. My name was written in polite font. I was now a suspect. I couldn't face reading any further and threw the phone across the room.

I needed a disguise. Applying the violet paste to my scalp, I sat in the baking heat until the hair bleached bright white. The smell was furious. Through the window of the motel, I saw the body of a silver UFO lost above scorched Reno, the white faces of rats looking up from their dust-ridden concrete bunkers. I practised speaking with a new voice in the mirror, a few octaves lower. The room was slow and quiet. It translated the hum of the traffic into its own rhythm. I recorded my new voice and played it back to me.

I had tried to locate Kaylee on Facebook and Instagram but was unable. I looked through photographs from local wrestling events. Men screaming in Lycra shorts, making a pantomime of their own clownish bodies in a vaudevillian game of dominance-submission. Men are such apes. Under the cold tap of the bathroom, I washed away the strong stench of bleach. Afterwards, I applied the second, gold paste. I was a sunflower stood in a field of Japanese blood. I remembered Tokyo again and visiting a strip club in the Shinjuku district. It had a red curtain pulled across the doorway. Inside, women danced under ultraviolet lights amongst marijuana plants growing towards the ceiling. Men were tied to the walls and flogged with tasselled whips. Their skin had started to bruise along the thighs in soft pink welts. A woman stood in nothing but a silver thong, introduced herself, and took me into a dark booth. There was a vending machine in the corner of a cramped space filled with large sex toys. The intimacy of her body towered over mine, closer to that of an electrical pylon. It was like living on the moon.

"Make a wish," the dominatrix said.

We were unable to touch, but she made a transmission from a different planet. Radiation blasted through blind space. Closing my eyes, she lowered a line of spit from her mouth into mine. Blonde. I was reborn. Being a model is about being invisible. You walk in front of the camera because you don't really exist. I had learned this in my earlier years. What desire demands is often your complete disappearance. I wanted to stand at the end of the Mojave Desert and face a nuclear detonation. The red wall of Armageddon smeared across peroxide skulls. I wanted to rub my gums in gunpowder because my dreams were my only companions now. They carried with them a navigation of nocturnal violence. I was finally alone with my dreams.

In the Marc Jacobs sunglasses, I packed a small bag to make my way to the 7th & Carson Café. Walking through the downtown street, I was an alien lost inside an argenteum paradise. Silver arcades and horizontal endless limousines. Gymnasiums filled with anabolic machines. I walked past a fluorescent sex shop: silicone weapons, a floppy dildo see-sawing in the window, a beautiful trans woman covered in a red latex cobweb. A zip that opened into her mouth. Lingerie. Mannequins decked in silver wear: grenades, an Uzi strapped to the wet hole of a fuck doll. I painted my eyes blue and shut. I applied enormous eyelashes. They looked like butterflies. I wanted to mutilate everything.

15.

Golden clouds broke across the oceanic skull of a stranger as the northern hemisphere of grey cumulus sank lower, moving closer now to roofs and the cluster of magnolia apartment blocks that made up the busy junction. Towards the west rose a large tower with the words *Bank of America* written in electric blue font. The café that Kaylee had written down was at an intersection between two busy roads. At the traffic light, I stopped to lower the strap of my Manolo Blahnik stiletto that was rubbing at the base of my calf. I had dressed up for her in the mango yellow Léger dress and some plain silver hoops. A human body can become a monolith. Smiling, I applied small crescents of cobalt Charlotte Tilbury eyeshadow like the frontage of some exotic bird. I carried a jagged knife inside my heart, the scowl of a hyacinth macaw.

In the taxi downtown, I silently witnessed a turkey vulture in an empty parking lot tear open the body of a smaller rock pigeon. A death-dance of feather and blood. Soon, there was nothing but a soiled pool: oil and dirt. I smelled like gasoline. I wasn't wearing any knickers in the taxi. It was exciting to dress up for Kaylee. I have always felt like a doll. Even as a child, whenever my mother would spit at me and scream, the impact of her words and her venom simply never really occurred. Because I wasn't there. It was like screaming at a lamp or a chair.

On winter nights, I would look at my husband as he served our children bowls of steaming rice. It was like a bad advertisement I had drifted inside. You start out in life and it spreads around you, as slow and fully as lichen, and then it presents itself to you *as your own*. People become proud of the delusions they have fostered for no reason. When I began to get migraines, I saw all life as sickness. I continued to work, but I was living inside a sparkling grotto filled with marionettes. I wanted to escape. But to commit a crime, one must speak with the voice of another. One must wake up one morning, and dress very calmly, and make their way towards a door. Through the doorway, one would find an empty hallway, a conservatory flooded with false suns.

"Why, good afternoon, ma'am. Are you here for food or just drinks? And can I ask, have you made a reservation?"

The maître d' was a young woman, striking in her innocent looks. She looked out of place like she should be working on a farm somewhere. A small and amber door mouse. She signalled to the half-empty restaurant. Through an open set of patio doors lay a wooden decked courtyard filled with tables and green oak saplings. The sound of traffic beyond was calming. I could smell meat being cooked from a nearby open grill.

"I'm meeting a friend here, *Kaylee*. She made a reservation for twelve noon."

"Let me just look at that for you," the girl replied, scrolling through the list of names on her iPad, which hung on a Velcroed belt around her waist.

"Yes, a booking here for a Kaylee at twelve noon. She booked for you both to sit outside. Is that OK?"

I nodded and followed the server to a table in the far corner of the patio. The heat had already solidified into a powerful, bright square. I was grateful to be seated beneath the saplings, where I could smell their broken leaves inside the thick, mauve shade. The maître d' asked if I wanted a glass of wine to which I declined. She brought me a carafe of water.

I sat and waited. I was hungry but didn't order anything. I looked down at my beautiful legs in the Manolo Blahniks laced up past the ankle. As the hour dragged by, I felt the eyes of others move along those diagonal insectile limbs of mine.

"Was there a phone number for the reservation?" I asked, to which the girl checked on her iPad. She shook her head. This time, I took up her offer of wine. I hadn't brought much money with me in my purse, only about fifty dollars. I was running short on cash. There was a little bit more at the hotel.

I emptied the dollar bills from my purse onto the table and pushed them across to the server, asking her to bring me a bottle and the keep the rest. The wine was served cold in a silver bucket. I held it close to my face, feeling the clarity and coldness of the neck of the bottle. Pouring it into the large glass, it tasted like pale apples falling through air. My heart and blood loosened with the intake of alcohol. I looked at other couples as they devoured plates of steak and beetroot, their mouths spread wide like basking sharks as they engulfed pink forkfuls of plasma-ridden rocket, the iron-rich flesh.

It had been over an hour and a half. Kaylee wasn't coming. I poured out the rest of the bottle and threw it into my mouth. I suddenly felt the alcohol hit me. I hadn't eaten all morning. Deep inside my gut, I knew that Kaylee wanted to come. She had made the reservation but not arrived. When we spoke, there was a deep and profound connection. Leaving the restaurant, I waved goodbye sadly to the maître d', who waved back.

"I hope you find your friend," she said, smiling and turning to a new customer entering past me.

These words implanted themselves within me like bright seeds. I saw myself inside the red vortex of the hotel room, making love to Kaylee, the hot desert air pouring through the air vents. Kaylee was above me like a poltergeist on fire. Afterwards, she had taken off her dress and shown me the scars along the inside of each shoulder. She had to be cut out of a car wreck at the age of seventeen by nine paramedics. The knife had left marks down each side of her back. I tongued them madly and then between her legs and buttocks. Her face in the darkness was like Celine, a planet sank beneath a deep, dark pool. I saw her brutish boyfriend screaming in her face, locking the door of their hotel room and forbidding her to leave this morning. I saw his handsome, piggish face as he swigged cans of Pabst Blue Ribbon and watched men on the small television leaping from the ropes of a wrestling ring onto each other. Grown men in bright green Lycra. Kaylee was crying in the bathroom.

The rage was rising inside my chest. Urgency floated above my solar plexus like a flower. At the intersection of the four roads, cars screamed through pollution as the lights switched into amber. Every car on the road paused and waited for me to dance through the street. There was a hesitation to each and every action in this universe. Swinging the purse around my perfect body, I reached for the mobile phone and ran down the street to the nearest alleyway. Tears were welling in my eyes. My breath was laboured. It was so simple to find the number and hear the voice of the sensible man in his sensible office. I instantly felt calmer and certain of how necessary this all was now, making the phone call.

"Hello, Mr Garcia." I said, staring at a white Toyota parked in the street, "I need to buy a firearm."

16.

I was running low on cash but took out the last $2000 for the gun. I knew the authorities would be able to locate me at the cashier desk. I signed the slip and handed it over. The cashier was a young Mexican man with a large, handsome face. He handed the bills back to me and fed the signed sheet back into the speechless ATM machine.

On the street outside, the faces of others had taken on a strange symmetry, their bodies forming a long palindrome towards the afternoon sun like a blurred queue of meat beneath the emerald backs of vultures flying through the city. Hot winds rose up from open sewer grates, bringing with them the subterranean graveyard smells of downtown Las Vegas. I wandered beneath fluorescent cowboys that cocked their hats at each other. They wore bulging cod pieces. The cowboys were gatekeepers to an impossible Platonic world behind the façade of these buildings and casinos, where lay the promise of an endless and flat land that moved from the outskirts of its crystalline streets into the blank desert beyond. Lines of golden palm trees rose up from the dead earth. Neon intergalactic shapes hovered above the nearby hotel: a green dollar bill, an azure cocktail glass with a ruby-bright maraschino cherry. Down the road roared a banana-yellow Mazda MX-5.

I had planned to meet the associate of Mr Garcia, at a restaurant in one of the quieter streets off Fremont, but it was impossible to avoid the crowds. I entered the busy Five Guys, only to be quickly attacked by a hostess. She was an older lady. Her hair had faded purple beneath the greasy snapback. A silver chain around her throat was stuck with sweat to the tired, freckled skin.
"We are struggling to find seats at this time, am afraid. Unless you got a reservation, of course."

I didn't respond or glance back at her. I could

feel the repetition of her hot breath. *In. Out. In. Out.* Looking across the sea of beelike diners that swarmed and fed off each other, a deep revulsion washed over me and twisted inside my stomach. They passed handfuls of bread back and forth to their mouths in a perverse and unknowable ritual. A bottle of malt vinegar had been knocked over at some point and left a brown strain across the white counter behind the hostess. Children, like chimpanzees, leaped up from their chairs and threw the sadness away from their bodies in large and mucky handprints.

It wasn't hard to spot the associate of Mr Garcia. He was sat at the table exactly as he had described, in an indigo dinner jacket. He had a dark head of hair. I pointed across at the man and walked straight past the hostess. I could feel my blood sugar starting to crash after the wine.

"Afternoon, Vanessa," said the associate, in an unknown European accent.

The man was wearing expensive sunglasses with a cheap shirt beneath the dinner jacket. The hair along his forearms and chest was coarse and black. His sideburns were shocking white. They eventually met his dark hair above the ear in coarse and tangled currents. Sitting across from him, I could see the hair was, in fact a toupee. The superglue was shining where it reached the perimeter of the sideburn. I raised my hand for a beer.

"Look, Vanessa. This will not take long. I suggest we keep it brief."

Lowering my hand, he patted the blue plastic bag that was next to him, tucked inside the booth, close to the wall.

"Is that it?" I asked, looking over, feeling my pulse quicken.

The children in the restaurant began to howl in unison.

"This place is a zoo, no?" said the associate, almost telepathically, looking around at the squabbling families, the empty faces of men and women peering down at their processed hamburgers, the empty polystyrene plates. "It's easy to be invisible in a place like this."

I smiled and nodded. I wanted to see the gun.

"OK, why the fuck not," said the associate suddenly, signalling for the waitress to come over. She was petite in a small blue apron, shirt, and skirt. The name badge read Grace. "A large beer for my friend, here. And I'll have the ice cream sundae."

After she left, we sat in silence for a few minutes. He never took his eyes off me. The ceiling fan spun above, distributing heat across the screaming room. The same waitress brought over the beer and ice cream.

"Grace," he said, pointing to the back of the waitress as she walked away, "That was my sister's name. She looked a lot like you. She was a very beautiful girl."

"Thank you," I replied, swigging down the first cold, frothy mouthful of beer.

"Do you like to fuck?" he said in a matter-of-face manner, his mouth full of pink-white ice cream. "If you're struggling for cash then I know a few guys that would pay $3000 a night. All the cocaine you want."

"I'm fine for money," I lied, the coldness of the beer running through me.

"You sure are a pretty thing. Damn! Out here, too, all alone. And needing this," he said, patting the blue bag. "You must be in all kinds of trouble, baby girl."

I looked down. I thought about reaching for the bag and blowing his brains out across the wall. His brains might resemble the faint stain of vinegar along the counter. Or possibly the stain inside Celine's apartment. I saw his entire skull expand around the chamber of the gun.

"Ice cream. You got a favourite flavour?" he asked.

"What?" I said, exasperated, finally returning his stare.

"You know vanilla, chocolate, pistachio. There are so many goddamn flavours."

I didn't reply. I continued to drink my beer, wishing him to leave. Eventually, he got the message and stood up from the booth. A shiver moved through my back as he placed a hand on my shoulder and brought his face close down to mine. I could smell the sweet and pungent sugar on his breath.

"You ain't no killer, little girl. You're just an orchid in a cesspit. And no flower like you can survive in this desert."

After he left, I felt the blood rush in large and warm waves. Afternoon light crashed through the vertical blinds across the greasy windows of the restaurant. Sadly, I ate the rest of his ice cream. The cacophonous children continued to scream, unable to verbalise the pain and sorrow they carried from day to night, offering themselves finally, at dusk, to the emptiness of sleep, a lullaby from their mother's small mouth—their daily gateway into oblivion. Rising from the booth, I reached out my hand towards the plastic bag and felt the gun inside. I instantly felt calmer.

17.

For the following two days, I remained low. I wandered from the motel to the local bus station and checked the faces of transient ghosts as they drifted through automatic doors into pale blue bus stands. There was a fashion store opposite the station that had gone out of business. It was filled with mannequins with crushed limbs that had fallen against the base of the window in a tangled mess. Their broken bodies were piled high. Polythene covers hung from empty hangers, floating in the centre of the main room. The floor was littered with cardboard and dirt. Outside, a desert wind blew sand across the large pavements.

That morning, I walked in the opposite direction of the city, making my way north along Route 604. Passing an airbase, there were about five stationary thunderbirds: red-white-blue metal planes resting on the boiling concrete. I came to the end of a military zone and looked out at the bare brushland. The land was filled with the skeletal remains of cattle and birds, necrophiliac insects, and amber rust. The land fed on the bleached bones of the dead. From the airbase, machines were sent into the sky to explode into laser-guided missiles, nocturnal soldiers illuminated on their monitor screens as green shapes, gnomes crawling along a sand dune.

Lost in this silent and horizonal land, the hot air stole the living breath from your mouth. I was missing England. Here, a snakelike arm of heat moved through your entire body. On the endless afternoon, I was lying on my bed in the motel, daydreaming of Kaylee. I tipped my head back and opened my mouth, allowing the serpentine current of warmth to re-enter. I would speak to myself, thoughts falling from my mouth like gobstoppers, enormous and purple fantasies that bounded across the marble floor. Taking the gun out of the plastic bag, I drew an outline of Ryan against the bathroom mirror and aimed the trigger straight at his chest. The cylinder of the weapon would fling his internal organs apart like a magician's bouquet. I saw him tied to a chair in a warehouse, his hair smoothed down. Snivelling, he wept at the foot of a large statue. It was the statue in the London hotel. It was the statue of a boy. Ryan was very still. There was a kitchen knife lodged inside his throat.

Another day past. The rooms of the hotel were filthy. I was noticing this more the longer I stayed. I tried to not to look at the dark crust around the bottom perimeter of the wall. When the maid came in, an old woman from Puerto Rico, she looked at me dumbfounded.

"Fire ants," I began to pant, "In the bathroom faucet."

Laughing, she left the room. I was just another hysterical gringo.

I had 50 dollars left in cash and unable to go to the bank again. It was too risky. In the oversized sunglasses, I walked to one of the bodegas downtown. It took me over three hours for the roundtrip. The streets were filled with men that looked like Ryan. They exercised all morning to beat their wives in the evening. Their arms were covered in mindless tattoos like the scribblings of an overstimulated toddler. Handing over the fifty-dollar bill to the cashier, I pointed at the large bottle of tequila on the top shelf. Taking the bottle and paying the man, I turned to leave, when there he was. Ryan stood in yellow Lycra. It was a poster on the bodega wall for an amateur wrestling event.

XTREME WRESTLING SMACKDOWN.

He was standing with about a dozen other men. The day and time of the poster was tonight. Unscrewing the bottle, I downed a large mouthful. The alcohol was clear and perfect.

It wasn't difficult to break into the empty clothes shop across from the bus station. There was a wooden panel nailed to the back of the building that you could pull away with little effort. Inside, there was not much stock left. I kicked around empty pieces of cardboard. In the office, I found no money left in any of the drawers. Maybe I was being indulgent since I had a bundle of clothes at the hotel, but I wanted something new. The feeling of putting on a new dress was like nothing else.

I kept the rest of the bottle of tequila in my purse. Inside the unbearable heat of Nevada, I was like an assassin floating above the fortress walls of the Alcazaba of Almería. At night, I dreamed of Celine asleep on a bed of Spanish roses. Black oil was flowing through her empty head. Frustrated, I kicked in a locked door in the back office, where I finally found the few remaining clothes. They were all garish. I tore them away from the hangers until I found the one suitable gown. A white cotton Totême dress with a crocheted belt. Simple, unassuming. Dragging it from the room, I made sure not to mark the gown as I crawled back through the hole in the wall, holding the dress close to me like a secret lover. A virgin saved from carnivalesque squalor, brought home from the sad tropics.

Back at the hotel, I changed quickly but took my time to apply my makeup. I had showered slowly, and cleaned under my armpits and even douched with the shower nozzle. I had spent the afternoon staring at the empty pool at the back of the hotel. Pale moss was growing along the insides of the tiles in dark lines. When I checked my phone, I made sure not to read any updates about the murder investigation. There had been a video of Celine's nephew weeping outside a north London home. His mother, Celine's sister, didn't say a word. She simply looked past the camera. I was eating a bag of salted chips in front of the television. I saw the death of the universe as an indigo-bloodied corpse stripped and tied to a telegraph pole.

It was time to go. I placed the handgun in my purse. Inside the blue plastic bag was a silencer that I screwed into the top of the gun before leaving the hotel room. In the hallway mirror, I stopped and drew on a final outline of lipstick.

"Excuse me, *Vanessa*," Charlie said mockingly from behind the reception desk as I made my way through the motel lobby. Inside my handbag, I had the gun, sunglasses, and the bottle of tequila. The white dress was shining against my tanned skin. "Huh?" I replied abruptly, not wanting to be distracted.

A smile deepened in Charlie's face, showing the translucent nerves beneath the skin. There are moments in life when a human face reveals its history. Hers was like a powerful grid. Beneath the silk shirt, I could see she wasn't wearing a bra again. She pointed to the computer screen which she turned towards me gently. On the screen was another article from an American newspaper, some local rag called Boulder City News. *Officials Trace London Killer to Las Vegas.* There was a large photograph of my face, a modelling shot from about four years ago.

"What a beautiful girl," Charlie snorted. "Does she look familiar to you?"

I tried to ignore and block out the situation for a moment. But she continued to laugh. I was nervous and looked around quickly at who was in hearing distance. The other guests continued to swim through the warm lobby towards the poolside, where the blinding water hit their arch and lean bodies. Inside the shock of the silver water, they all resembled hammerhead sharks.

"What do you want?" I asked calmly, feeling my hand shudder towards the purse.

"Cash," she replied, instantly. She had rehearsed this conversation. Her tone was polished and confident. "I need $10,000 by midnight, or else I phone the cops."

Stunned, I looked over the glasses at the girl. Her mouth tightened with resolve.

"Can we discuss this?' I asked, signalling to the small office behind the reception. A radio was blaring loudly inside, a modern pop song I didn't recognise.

"Sure," she said, moving backwards into the room, turning the computer screen back to its original position. Smiling, she knew she had conquered me and was enjoying the act of playing with her food. I signalled to the chair and asked her if I could smoke. Again, she seemed relaxed and agreed. I offered her one, and she accepted. The music was screaming from the radio.

"I can get the money for you tonight," I assured her, wanting to deescalate. The music had grown even louder on the radio. I pulled out the bottle of tequila, and she began to laugh.

"You lady are one fucking nutjob."

I laughed, too, and offered her the bottle from which she swigged. She rested the cigarette in her lips. I began to feel in the front pocket of the handbag.

"I don't have a lighter," I said, "Is there one in here?"

"Jeez, *Vanessa*. So, why did you kill that woman then, huh? Was she not into you? Or was she married with kids? I know your type," she smirked.

"I've seen the way you look at my tits. Fucking lesbians."

"I bet there's a lighter in those drawers over there."

I signalled to the office desk.

Charlie continued to laugh and turned away to look. I could feel the rage inside me rising. As a child, I would always have migraines during thunderstorms. My mother would only be kind to me when there was a storm. She would hold me closely and tend to me like a poor animal. And from the window, we would watch blue electricity come down in a torrent of miraculous energy. Heaven suddenly connected to the world.

"You stupid bitch," I said, pulling out the revolver and firing two bullets into her back.

The first bullet entered her left shoulder, and she staggered forwards a few steps, as though blinded and confused. For the second, I aimed slightly higher into the back of her head, sending her brains out all across the filing cabinet. Her arms jolted open from the shock of the impact as she fainted forwards into the metal piece of furniture. Afterwards, she slumped lifelessly on the floor. The music continued blaring loudly from the machine. *My love is like a rocket. Watch it blast off. And I'm feeling so electric, dance my arse off.* The silencer on the revolver had muffled the gunshot. No one would have heard over the music. It wasn't difficult to drag Charlie's body into the janitor's cupboard at the back of the office and throw it beneath a pile of black trash bags. I used some of the tequila on a clean rag to wipe away the blood smeared across the filing cabinet. Around her waist were a set of keys to the reception till. Peering out of the door, I waited until the reception cleared. In the till was about $4,300, which I emptied into my handbag. On the computer screen was still my photograph. I took the mouse and scrolled up to the close window. I pressed the small X in the corner. Time to leave Sunset Creek.

18.

The parking lot of the wrestling arena was like a furnace of heat and gravel. A burning yellow square of gargantuan, diesel-chugging 4x4s where men stood in small cliques, guzzling cans of red-blue Budweiser. Their arms were sleeved in Japanese dragons, vague voodoo, and other stereotypically vague biker fare. They had pig bright faces and wore silver handlebar moustaches. A pair of bull dykes leaned against the far brick wall. I watched them pass a cigarette back and forth between their muscular faces, their jaws as lean as pit-bulls.

I kept the money stolen from the motel sealed in my purse and jacket pockets. It wouldn't all fit inside the purse. Every time a police siren went past, I felt this weight inside my stomach. It was like a dark stone. I bought myself a black Carhartt baseball cap and tucked my hair up tightly in a bun. In the oversized sunglasses, I sank down low into my seat. I had been waiting for over three hours in the baking Mondeo I rented under a fake name.

A few men suddenly came to the door of the car and tapped on the window. One of them asked if I was selling benzos or weed.

"I'm just waiting for a friend," I smiled at the orc-like biker, the rancid smell of him hitting me as I lowered the window, letting in an unspeakable wall of heat and dust.

"Sure, lady," he replied, bursting into laughter, his eyes red from the mixture of beer and weed.

Thankfully, he quickly returned to the opposite side of the parking lot. Two muscular security guards were on the doors at the entrance to the building. When they glanced over, I pulled out a paperback book I found in the glove box. A chick-lit novel. I tried not to make eye contact with anyone.

Earlier on, when I had first arrived at the arena and parked up, I instantly recognised them both. Ryan was signing his autograph for a weedy teenager at the entrance, a pathetic boy with a vest that said YES BRO on. The boy was gushing over Ryan. Kaylee was turned to the side, looking bored and scrolling through her phone. She looked just how I remembered. Her warm and open face. She looked exactly like Celine.

"Excuse me, ma'am," a sudden knock at the window again, which startled me. It was one of the security guards. "Ma'am this lot is only for customers of the venue."

"Hi," I said, rolling down the window, looking up at the minotaur of a man. "I'm just waiting for a friend. Could I stay here a little longer?"

"Fraid not," he answered, sharpy. "Them's the rules. You got a problem with rules, lady?"

Smiling, I shook my head and raised the window, before starting the engine.

Thankfully, I could park on the opposite side of the main street after finding some change for the meter. I waited until sundown. Intoxicated men and women staggered along the sidewalk, linking arms and falling down onto the warm stone. A billboard above the arena showed the poster of over three hundred amateur wrestlers, and soon, these same men began to leave the building. A small crowd of fans, mostly meathead gym types, stood around to shake hands with the wrestlers. Getting out of the car, I tried to decipher the flow of bodies. The faces of the wrestlers had changed since entering, some were now covered in cuts and purple bruises. One had a swollen lip. It was hard to make out Ryan or Kaylee. Finally, they emerged from the arena doors after about twenty minutes. Ryan looked no different. He smiled that large and artificial grimace. He yanked Kaylee with him by the elbow towards the other side of the parking lot, where they got into a small, cheap-looking car. As they set off, I slowly started the Mondeo and began to follow them.

The city sky grew darker in sailboats of confused violet clouds. My car swam after theirs through the fluorescent arcades decorated in sin and pleasure. A green oasis of xenon light. Their car was swerving in and out of traffic and it was difficult to keep up at times. They stopped at a traffic light, and my heart began to beat faster as I came up behind them. We were so close. I wanted to reach into their bodies with the car and the gun. Light above faltered and started to seizure from endless telegraph poles, the symmetrical casinos that lit up faces of people in the filthy street, each bewildered by the Martian glow of the store windows. Frozen in the car seat, in my baseball cap and sunglasses, I was slowly becoming translucent in this vast metropolis, a holographic vampire.

Amber strips of dusk folded into voracious night. The night in the desert wanted to consume everything and hovered like a vulture above the bones of the living that rode in elevators up to their lonely rooms and wept inside crystalline apartments, drinking from decanters and tumblers filled with bronze shining bourbon. Ryan's car suddenly indicated down a road through the sleazier part of downtown. The vehicle wept inside a halo of rainbows. The ends of Kaylee's hair was flowing from the open window. Outside the doorway of two adjacent nightclubs, three beautiful girls stood in red bikinis and large stilettos. They smoked cigarettes and laughed in bright clouds of smoke.

The car had slowed down now and pulled into an alleyway suddenly. It was unexpected, so I had to reverse quickly, causing a bus behind to beep his horn. Accelerating, I turned the car to follow. I thought I had lost them but soon I saw the beat-up old car at a motel opposite and Ryan trying to find his keys. It was the end apartment on the ground floor. Number 22. I smiled and waited for darkness to engross every room in the city. It covered and smothered their sleeping bodies. Its hatred was inevitable.

19.

I had gone to a local bar on the next block to build up my courage. A dank hovel made of sandstone and wooden beams. There was a hole in the wall that opened to a foul-smelling shelter where obese bikers played cards and smoked heroin. They each had Roman numerals tattooed on their arms. Someone had drawn the image of a green snake on the far wall above the card table. Its single eye glowed inside the dark room, golden and alone. "Another Jim Beam," I spluttered at the tender behind the granite ledge. The bartender's vision appeared poor, and he felt loudly for the bottles that rattled on their shelves, until eventually he found the smooth shape of the correct bottle at the end. He poured me a shot and then another. Afterwards, I took a beer to the far corner and waited until it was time for us all to leave. There was a couple slow dancing in the corner, both inebriated. They folded their limbs around each other like wet laundry. I watched them waltz from the bar out into the pale and empty desert.

"Closing time," said the bartender, struggling to peer through the room with his vague alabaster sight.

As a child, my grandfather suffered from parasites that had somehow entered his bloodstream. My mother showed me images of his retinas, like veined and orange planets—photographs brought home from the eye doctor. Sat in my grandfather's terraced house, I imagined his retina stretched across the ancient sky amongst tombstone grey clouds, each organ sensing the slow tide of ingestion beneath. A parasite was eating from the capillaries into the red retina pulled as tight as a drum.

I was drunk enough by that point to return once more to the parking lot in front of the apartment—number 22. The lights were still on in the back, which I assumed was the kitchen and the bathroom. There was a light visible at the front.

The revolver in my pocket weighed heavily. Dust was rising in thick currents around my Nike Air Max trainers. I had changed out of the white dress in the bar restroom into thin, dark clothes. Time moved slowly across the gentle song of insects, their purring sleep. I reached for the door of their apartment and it opened instantly, unlocked. I could see the blue stream of the television as it hit the walls of the living room. The light washed along the sublime profile of Kaylee's face. A cigarette brought to her lips was caught in a silver lullaby of smoke that flickered inside the shimmering screen. Suddenly, her zoetrope face turned towards me, and the mouth fell open to see the figure stood at the door.

"Ryan!" she yelled, moving to the opposite door, where her partner appeared in nothing but a towel. His hair was wet from the shower, his chest covered in illegible tattoos. He had modelled himself on Brazilian gangsters.

"Who the fuck are you?" he laughed, turning to Kaylee and then back to me again. I pushed the door close with my foot. "Is she the maid? No more towels, OK? Do you people ever fucking knock?"

"It's the woman from the Palazzo!"

His laugher grew louder and tore through the room. He went into the next room as though he didn't care.

"What is she doing here?" Kaylee pleaded as she followed him into the kitchen. I moved after them slowly, as though a monster invited into a haunted castle. I stood at the doorway as they argued and fought beneath the buzzing kitchen light. Insects were batting themselves against the acrylic bulb with mottled brown wings in a blind and endless dance. He looked like he was frying a piece of meat on the stove. She reached and grabbed his arm tightly.

"Look lady," he spoke with his back turned to me, prodding the meat aimlessly with a fork, "I don't know why you came here, but I suggest you fuck off back to whatever hole you crawled out of."

I pulled the revolver from my jacket pocket. Kaylee began to scream. I suddenly saw the animal confusion in her face. The safety clicked. When Ryan turned, he saw the gun, too. His veneered teeth hovered in the ultraviolet light.

"Kaylee," I said calmly to the girl, "You can come with me."

Ryan burst loudly into roaring laughter. The smell of grease filled the kitchen.

"You hear that, you can go with her!" His face hardened now and became tense. I rose the gun from his chest and aimed neatly at his face. "Why don't you tell her, Kaylee? What we get up to here, huh? These sick little games. How we pick up men and women from casinos and steal their money. Especially dumb fucking dykes flaunting their cash at casino bars who probably—"

The gun went off in his face and splattered bone and blood across the tiled wall above the stove. The meat was still smoking in the pan, the grease darkening into a rich gravy. I could see Kaylee shaking in the corner of the room. Breathless, she didn't speak when I moved to the bathroom and tore down the shower curtain. I began to wrap the naked body in the vinyl sheet. We had to move quickly. She reached trembling for her phone, which I took from her hands and placed in my pocket. She gave me another bewildered look.

"Grab his feet," I ordered.

She tried to run, but I held the gun at her. Shaking uncontrollably, she took the base of the body. Looking from the door, there were no cars around as we moved quickly to the back of the rented Mondeo. I had to fold up the knees to fit him completely inside. I locked Kaylee in the front when I made my way back to the apartment and quickly wiped the walls with water and bleach. I rubbed all the door handles with my sleeve. Suddenly, the smoke alarm began to wail above my head. It announced the panic sitting inside my chest. It was a relief to hear the siren. The machine spoke a cold language I was unable.

20.

Soundless grey sand. I could smell the girl had urinated herself in the front seat of the car. Stuttering, she pleaded her case to me. She told me how they had planned the whole argument and how they often picked up men and some women at the casino. Her whole *damsel in distress* bit. A beat-up whore in need of a shining knight. She told me that back at my motel, I never opened the safe, so she never got a chance to learn the code. "But the next day, we never showed up because I told Ryan to leave you alone. You gotta believe me, lady. You gotta."

I smiled and nodded, and turned back to the

steering wheel.

We drove from Apex to Dry Lake to Crystal, and then further into the desert. We watched Las Vegas recede behind the car like an imaginary city. A geyser of light spewed upwards into permanent twilight. Condors circled above in smooth and effortless tornadoes. Death was the language of the desert. Buried deep beneath the Alcazaba of Almería, Spanish corpses of knights slept in cobwebbed glass cases under pyramids of powder blue skulls.

I looked so beautiful in the wing mirror, even then. It was like I had lived my entire life in a magazine. Celine's bedroom had one of David Hockney's collages of the Mojave Desert nailed to the wall. *Pearblossom Highway* from April 1986. When I looked across at Kaylee, she looked almost like my daughter in the reptile house. Her breath quickened. Her face was bathed in the flashing red light of the indicator as I pulled into a dark layby. We had to move quickly to get the body away from the road.

Sweat was pouring from our foreheads. The sand and dirt were so heavy to pull away with our fingers. Without a shovel, it took us over two hours. The sand kept falling back into the hole. The sand moved in constant, invisible rhythms, betraying itself as it returned instantly to the areas we pulled away from. Kaylee was sobbing loudly as we threw the corpse into the ground.

Light began to break in orange waves across the distant horizon as dawn ran through her frenzied blonde hair. I wanted to kiss her mouth. I thought of Celine and Lucia riddled with beautiful knives. "You don't need to do this," the girl muttered as I raised the gun towards her. I could see she was about to get hysterical and run. "I can be whatever you want me to be."

The gun fired one shot into her chest, and she fell facedown onto the body. It simply looked like she had fainted in the sweltering heat of the morning. I thought of white dwarf stars in their last moments as they extinguish themselves in a burst of lavender breath. It is so easy to end. Nothing now but the purple moon struggling behind its veiled clouds and the surrounding buildings propped up in pools of blank quicksand, broken walls lost amongst spears of bright yucca.

Looking at my shirt and arms, I realised I was covered in Kaylee's blood. It glowed brighter now in the red rising sun. Moving to the opposite side of the grave, I wiped my hands on a marigold bush. The orange plasma glistened across its yellow petals. I pushed large handfuls of dirt over the two bodies. The sand felt warm in my embrace. Sweating even more, it took a further twenty minutes to cover them both.

Placing the revolver back inside my jacket pocket. I took a bottle of Evian from the car and washed my face and hands. The water felt cool. I got back into the car and drove a further forty miles north. The morning rushed blue and warm through the windows of the vehicle. The golden sand expanded endlessly beneath the azure sky, which smashed itself on the windscreen like an offering: the breast of a bird murdered upon the hard and mahogany dashboard. Eventually, the car made a gurgling sound, and I realised it had run out of petrol. I was finally alone. I changed back into the cool white dress. I took the revolver, the fake passport, a few dollar bills, the remaining Evian and placed them into my Hermès purse. I should probably sell that at some point.

Out in the desert, the heat was unbearable. I wandered all morning until finally, I came to a small patch of stone houses. There was a garage and a bar. I ordered myself a large glass of water with ice cubes that I held in my burning mouth. A door flapped open and close at the end of the bar, leading back into the desert.

"What are you doing all the way out here, pretty thing?"

The man was older with thick dark hair. His face was handsome with sad blue eyes. He asked me about my accent and where I came from. He wanted to know everything about me. I told him I was a dentist from West Hollywood.

"I gave Julianne Moore some dental x-rays once. I removed her *maxillary incisor*," I said, tapping the top left canine. His face lit up, impressed. I explained that my car had broken down about ten miles south. He said he could drive there and help me get it towed back up to the garage. The man even offered a place to stay.

I went to the bar toilet to clean myself up. I still had smears of dirt down the backs of my forearms. I had three more bullets in the gun. The door of the bar continued to shake in the wind. It flung itself open inside the hot air. It mimicked the breath of the desert: delirious, alone. I walked outside and followed the dark shape of the man to his car.

Matthew Kinlin lives and writes in Glasgow. His published works include *Teenage Hallucination* (Orbis Tertius Press, 2021); *Curse Red, Curse Blue, Curse Green* (Sweat Drenched Press, 2021); *The Glass Abattoir* (D.F.L. Lit, 2023); *Songs of Xanthina* (Broken Sleep Books, 2023) and *Psycho Viridian* (Broken Sleep Books, 2024).

www.ingramcontent.com/pod-product-compliance
Lightning Source LLC
LaVergne TN
LVHW092048060526
838201LV00047B/1297